Fans are talking, texting, and blogging about Emma Chase and her *New York Times* and *USA Today* bestseller

Tangled

First in the sweet and sexy trilogy that includes
Twisted *and* Tamed
Chosen as one of Goodreads' 200
Most Popular Books of 2013

"Emma Chase will keep you enthralled and captivated. A brilliant 5 star read!!!!" (Neda, *The Subclub Books*) • "A brilliant, out-of-this-world hysterical, swoon-worthy five stars. Emma Chase's unforgettable characters are absolutely beyond compare. One of the best reads of 2013." (Tessa, *Books Wine Food*) • "It was absolutely amazing! Drew Evans is hands down my favorite leading man." (Liz, *Romance Addiction*) • "A 5-heart read. It's perfection in a book. RAWR hot, hilariously funny, and a romance so good you won't want it to end." (Tamie & Elena, *Bookish Temptations*) • "*Tangled* is panty-dropping, outrageously funny, and overwhelmingly lovely. I finished it in nearly one sitting because I had to know more of Drew and Kate." (Angie, *Smut Book Club*) • "Witty and hilarious insight into a man's head. I fell in love with Drew Evans's playful and cocky attitude and I will never forget him. . . . A sexy hero." (Lucia, *Reading Is My Breathing*) • "The characters are insanely hilarious! Drew had my sides splitting and in stitches with his witty and undeniably competitive personality! The funniest and most creative book told by the male point-of-view. You will not be able to put this book down!" (Stephanie, *Romance Addict E*

ALSO BY EMMA CHASE

Tangled

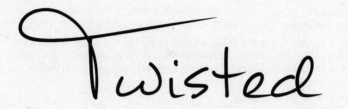

Twisted

Emma Chase

GALLERY BOOKS

New York London Toronto Sydney New Delhi

Gallery Books
A Division of Simon & Schuster, Inc.
1230 Avenue of the Americas
New York, NY 10020

First Gallery Books trade paperback edition March 2014

GALLERY BOOKS and colophon are registered trademarks of Simon & Schuster, Inc.

For information about special discounts for bulk purchases, please contact Simon & Schuster Special Sales at 1-866-506-1949 or business@simonandschuster.com.

The Simon & Schuster Speakers Bureau can bring authors to your live event. For more information or to book an event contact the Simon & Schuster Speakers Bureau at 1-866-248-3049 or visit our website at www.simonspeakers.com.

Manufactured in the United States of America

10 9 8 7 6 5 4 3 2

Library of Congress Cataloging-in-Publication Data

Chase, Emma
  Twisted / Emma Chase
     pages cm
1. Substance abuse—Fiction. 2. Relationship addiction—Fiction. 3. Lifestyles—Fiction. 4. Life change events—Psychological aspects—Fiction. 5. Solitude—Fiction. 6. Psychological fiction. I. Title.
PS3603.H37934T95 201423
813'.6—dc232013037284

ISBN 978-1-4767-6362-0
ISBN 978-1-4767-6363-7 (ebook)

Falling in love is easy, staying in love is hard.
Dedicated to all those who have stayed in love.

Acknowledgments

To the best agent a writer could ever ask for, Amy Tannenbaum, and to the whole Jane Rotrosen Agency team—I can't thank you enough for your wonderful guidance and encouragement; to my fantastic editor Micki Nuding and everyone at Gallery Books, including Kristin and Jules for their excitement and dedication. Thank you to the amazing Enn Bocci, for knowing just what to say at the right time and for always swinging for the fences. Endless appreciation to each of my online friends and to all the bloggers whose enthusiasm helped so many discover and fall in love with Drew Evans and Kate Brooks.

To my readers, for understanding and enjoying and having as much fun reading about these characters as I do writing them.

And I'm so very grateful for my brilliant husband and two beautiful children—thank you for your patience, love, and support, and for giving me a reason to smile every single day.

Twisted

Prologue

Women walk a fine line.
    Prude.
Slut.
Bitch.
Doormat.

Defining who you are to the outside world is a constant balancing act. It's exhausting. But for some women there is an occasional out. An excuse that lets them say what's really on their minds, allows them to forgive even if they know they shouldn't, and pushes them to indulge all those nasty little fantasies—without the scarlet consequences.

Alcohol.

It can give the courage to talk dirty and the permission to go home with the bartender.

It's the alibi. The cover story.

It wasn't really you—you were possessed by Captain Morgan and the Grey Goose.

Unfortunately, I have a very high tolerance for alcohol.

Sucks to be me.

In all our years together, Billy was never able to drink me under the table. Not once. Maybe it's because I started drinking at a young age. Maybe I was just born that way.

Regardless, it takes a lot to get me buzzed and even more to get me drunk.

That's why, back in the day, I preferred pot.

Much more efficient.

Yep, you heard me right. Kate Brooks—pothead extraordinaire. Me and the Grateful Dead? We could've been bestest friends. Weed courage is what made me brave enough to get my tattoo.

But, sadly, those days are over. As I started business school, I realized the consequences of getting caught with a controlled substance were just too high.

So now I stick to legally sanctioned drugs only. Mostly wine.

Drew and I drink it nightly, just to unwind. And once a week we have kind of a date night—a special night. We cook together. Drew is a big fan of the fajitas. We drink and talk and drink some more.

Tonight we drank a bit more than usual. So, even though I'm not wasted in the literal sense, my limbs feel loose. Relaxed. Just like my inhibitions.

Have I got your attention? Excellent.

Open a window, ladies and gents—it's about to get hot in here.

We're in bed.

I'm on my back. And Drew is between my legs.

Well—his face is, anyway.

"I love your pussy."

I moan, and he reinforces his words with actions. He's big on actions.

Wet, worshipful actions.

"I could fucking live down here."

He picks up his pace, and before you can say "Slap me with a riding crop," I'm pulling on his hair and screaming his name.

Moments later, Drew smirks proudly and crawls up my body. My limbs are lazy from the wine—and the orgasm, of course. All around, there's a pleasant haze, a mist of numbness, making everything seem dreamlike.

And then we're kissing. And heat spreads throughout my body like an electrical current, bringing me back.

Making me feel how real this is.

I rip my mouth from his and whisper—the alcohol making me brave—"Drew . . . Drew, I want to try something."

That gets his attention. "What do you want to try?" His tongue glides over my nipple.

I smile and bite my lip. "Something new."

He raises his head. His lids are adorably heavy. "I like new."

I chuckle and push him off me, then stand up and make my way toward the dresser—bumping into the nightstand as I go.

"Excuse me."

I open the top drawer and pull out two pairs of handcuffs. Delores got them for her post-wedding bachelorette party, but she already had a pair.

Don't ask.

I swing one around my finger. My sexy strut back to the bed is almost ruined as I stumble on my four-inch heels, and I giggle.

Drew rises up on his knees. He looks hungry, like a starving lion eyeing up a juicy steak that's just out of reach.

He moves to take the cuffs from me, but I push him away.

"On your back, big boy."

I know what he's thinking. Can't you almost hear him?

"Mmm . . . Kate wants to run the show? Interesting."

He backs up and brings his wrists to the posts of the headboard. I circle his wrists and lock the half moons in place.

Click.

Click.

He gives each one a tug, testing it out, as I rest on my heels beside him, my eyes smoothing over the rippling naked perfection that is Drew Evans.

Beautiful.

"You plan on doing something? Or are you just going to stare at me all night?"

I look up at him. And his eyes are eager, daring me to bring it on.

Oh, I can bring it. Don't ever doubt that.

I lift my chin proudly and bring my hands between his thighs. Rubbing and massaging his balls slowly. I slide my hand up his already hard cock, gripping it tight—the way I know he likes—before giving it a few firm pumps.

Drew's chest starts to rise faster.

Interesting indeed.

And before you ask, no, I wasn't always this way. This adventurous.

Bold.

My entire sexual relationship with Billy involved two levels: shy and mundane. Hesitant and rote. And that's just where it stayed. It was only after Drew that I realized how much Billy and I were holding each other back.

In sex—in life.

In each other's eyes, we would always be Katie and Billy. Immature. Dependent. Forever young—like that Tuck movie about the fountain of youth.

Then Drew Evans came into my life, and the outspoken, demanding, and yes, horny woman who had been growing inside me for a decade was set free. At least in bed.

His bed.

I bend at the waist, ass in the air, and take his length in with my mouth. He jerks at the contact. The alcohol must have numbed my gag reflex, because I'm able to take him all the way down my throat.

And I do.

Four, five, six times. Then I bring my eyes to his. During a blow job? Guys love eye contact. Don't ask me why—I have no idea.

"You like it when I suck your cock, Drew?"

He likes dirty talk too. Actually, there's not much Drew *doesn't* like.

His eyes roll back. "Fuck, yes."

I go back to work, letting my tongue get into the action.

His voice is breathy, panting. "God, baby—you give the best head. You could teach a frigging class."

Ha—that's funny! Dick Lick 101.

After almost two years together, I'm an expert at reading Drew's body language. So when his hips start to lift and his hands clench in the air, I know he's close. His appreciative grunts and groans almost make me abandon my plan.

But I don't.

At the last second, just before he comes, I pull away. And sit up. Drew's eyes are squeezed shut, waiting for the explosion that's not coming.

He opens his eyes and they're bewildered.

I smile, feeling empowered.

And naughty.

I yawn dramatically. "You know, that wine really took a lot out of me. I'm kind of tired."

"Wh . . . what?" he pants.

"I think I need a breather. You don't mind, do you?"

Drew growls, "Kate . . ."

I swing my leg over him, sliding his massively impressive hard-on between my legs. Sitting on it, but not letting it slip inside.

"I'm kind of thirsty too. I'm going to get a glass of water. You want some?"

"This isn't fucking funny, Kate."

Oooh, he's mad.

Scary.

I slide my finger down the middle of his chest. "Who's laughing?"

He pulls at the cuffs—harder this time. When the locks hold, I giggle. Who knew poking a lion with a stick could be so much fun?

"Relax, Drew. Stay put like a good boy and I'll come back . . ." I shrug. "Eventually."

I kiss his nose quickly, hop off the bed, and scurry from the room as he calls my name.

Don't look at me like that; I'm just teasing him a little. You know he deserves it. No harm in that, right?

$$\infty$$

I skip down the hall to the kitchen, proud of myself. When I step onto the cold tile floor, goose bumps rise up my legs and down my arms. I really am thirsty, so I get a glass from the cabinet and fill it with cold water.

Standing at the sink I take a nice long gulp, closing my eyes as the cool liquid soothes my dry throat. A drop trails down my chin, over my collarbone, and down my breast.

Without warning, a hard chest presses up against my back, shocking me. I squeak and the glass drops and shatters in the sink.

I don't know how he got free, but the handcuffs are dangling from his wrists. Rough hands pull me back, trapping me.

I shiver as seductive warm breath scrapes my ear.

"That wasn't nice, Kate. I can be not nice too."

His voice is low—not angry, but firm. It's incredibly arousing.

One hand grips my hair at the nape and pulls, making me arch my back and press my pelvis against the rim of the sink. He jerks my head to the side, and then he's kissing me—plunging his tongue into my mouth as I race to keep up.

The kiss is possessive.

Dominating.

A moment later he pushes easily inside me and starts a pounding rhythm, his lower abdomen slapping against my ass with each push.

It's exhilarating.

I hear myself moan. The counter bites into my stomach, but I don't care. All I can feel is Drew.

Controlling me. Driving me. Owning me.

His free hand grips mine and brings it around front to my clit. Pressing my fingers down, compelling me to pleasure myself.

Guys have a thing for masturbation. I've come to realize it's a huge turn-on—like throwing a match into a barrel of gasoline.

He releases my hand, but my fingers continue to move like he wants them to. Like I'm a puppet on a string, and Drew is the master puppeteer. And then he leans back, taking the heat of his chest away.

The pace of his thrusting slows. And I feel his hand slide down my spine. Between us.

To my ass.

His hand kneads and rubs, then his fingers glide around the mounds of flesh. Back and forth over the hypersensitive hole between them.

And I tense up.

This is new territory for us. Well—for me. I have no doubt that Drew has, at one time or another, been inside every available orifice of the female form.

But for me it's unknown. And a little nerve-racking.

His fingers make several harmless passes until I relax. Until the tension drains from my shoulders, and I'm once again distracted by the intense pleasure the rhythm of his hips invokes.

And then he slides one finger inside.

There's no pain. No discomfort. Double penetration is a lot like skydiving. To truly appreciate it, you have to experience it. Words don't really do it justice.

But I'll try: delicious.

In a forbidden, naughty kind of way.

Slowly Drew moves his finger in and out, catching up with the pace of his cock.

And I'm moaning, low and deep and uninhibited. My own fingers rub faster—harder—in front. Then I gasp as he stretches me wider, making room for the second finger he just slipped in.

His movements are unhurried. Torturous and teasing.

And I want to open my mouth and beg for more.

More friction, more heat.

Faster. More. *Please*.

Drew compels me forward gently. Bending me over, so my hair brushes the bottom of the sink. And then he's gone—out of my body.

And I ache with the loss of it.

Until I feel the head of his cock, wet with my fluids, stroking back and forth over the opening his fingers just occupied.

"Drew . . ."

It's a keening moan, half pleasure, half pain.

All pleading.

"Say yes, Kate. Fucking Christ . . . please say yes."

His voice is raspy. Raw.

With need.

For me.

And suddenly I feel powerful.

Strange, considering our current position, but still—I'm the one in control. He may as well be begging at my feet.

Waiting and hoping for my command.

I don't think. I don't weigh the options or contemplate the consequences. I only feel, submerged in rapturous sensation.

I let go.

And I trust.

"Yes . . ."

Ever so slowly, Drew presses forward into me. There's a moment of pain—a stretching burn—and I inhale sharply. He pauses. Until I release my breath. Then, gently, he continues forward, until his most intimate flesh is fully ensconced in my own. Then he stays completely still. Letting my body adjust to the intrusion.

I feel his hand slide across my hip and down my thigh, coming around to my front. His hand goes under mine, his fingers rubbing in a circular motion. In that sensuous, magnificent way, before dipping inside me. Over and over and over again.

I always thought of anal sex as the ultimate show of domination, forceful, maybe humiliating.

But this doesn't feel that way.

It's primal . . . unexplored . . . but beautiful too. Sacred.

Like I've just given him my virginity. And in a way, I guess I have.

I move first, pushing back against him.

Giving Drew permission—wanting to know, to experience these new sensations. Needing to cross the finish line. With him.

It's more than erotic. Beyond intimate.

Drew's lips press against the skin on my back. Kissing and cursing and whispering my name. And then he's the one moving. Taking back control. Gliding in and out—tender but steady.

It's divine.

My hand clasps over his at my clit. My legs tremble and I know I'm getting close. *So close.* Like climbing a mountain and realizing the peak is just mere steps away.

Our breaths come in deep, open-mouth pants with each drive of Drew's hips.

"Yes . . . yes . . . yes . . ."

Men's orgasms are ninety percent physical. It's easy for them to get off, regardless of where their thoughts are. Women have it harder. Our orgasms usually hinge on our mental state. Which means if you guys want to get us there? We can't be thinking about that load of laundry in the next room, or the pile of papers waiting on our desks.

Which explains why it's not Drew's hand, or dick, that does me in.

It's his voice.

With his forehead against my shoulder blade, he chants, "Oh God, oh God, oh God . . ."

It's so unlike him.

He sounds open. Exposed.

Vulnerable.

This infuriating man, who always wants to be in charge, calling the shots. Who doesn't make a move without examining it from every angle, turning it around in his amazing mind—the pros, the perks, the ramifications.

He's falling apart behind me.

And as he whispers a litany of profanities and prayers—I fall over the edge.

Into ecstasy.

My head snaps back and my eyes close. And stars burst behind my eyelids as I tense and scream, and wave after dizzying wave of pleasure wracks my body.

Drew's movements become uneven and jerky, more forceful and uncontrolled.

And a moment later he pulls my hips back against him, holding me there, as one long, last guttural moan spills from his lips.

Afterward, we catch our breaths. Still connected and quaking with aftershocks. His hands smooth up my arms as he slips out of me.

He turns me around to face him. His hands caress my cheeks, and then he's kissing me.

And it's so sweet. Kind and loving. Such a stark contrast to our desperate movements moments before.

I don't know why, but my eyes fill with tears.

Instantly, Drew's gaze turns worried. "Are you okay? Did I . . . did I hurt you?"

I smile through the tears, because they're happy ones. Because in some weird, unexplainable way, I've never felt closer to him than I do right now.

"No. I'm wonderful. Feel free to be not nice to me anytime."

Then he smiles too. Relieved and satisfied.

"Noted."

Drew picks me up and carries me to the shower. We stand under the warm spray and wash each other worshipfully. Then Drew wraps us in thick, heated towels and bears me to bed.

He pulls the blanket up over both of us and holds me tight against him.

And it makes me feel precious.

He makes me feel that way. Always.

Cherished.

Adored.

Was I sore the next day? A little. But it wasn't so bad.

Too much information?

Sorry. Just trying to be helpful.

In any case, the aches and pains of the following morning were more than worth it, as far as I was concerned.

But what's the point of all this, you ask? Why am I sharing it with you?

Because good sex? Really, really good sex?

Doesn't need alcohol. And it's not about compatibility, or practice, or even being in love.

It's about trust.

Letting your guard down. Putting yourself in another person's hands and letting him lead you to places you've never been before.

And I trusted Drew. With my mind, my heart, my body. I trusted Drew with everything.

At least I did then.

Chapter 1

In high school, biology was my favorite subject. What fascinated me most were species that transform into a whole new being. Like pollywogs. Or butterflies. They start out as one thing, but end up something else entirely.

Unrecognizable.

Everyone always looks at butterflies and thinks, "How lovely." But no one ever thinks about what they had to go through to become what they are. When the caterpillar builds its cocoon, it doesn't know what's happening. It doesn't understand that it's changing.

It thinks it's dying. That its world is ending.

The metamorphosis is painful. Terrifying and unknown. It's only afterward that the caterpillar realizes it was all worth it.

Because now it gets to fly.

And that's what I feel like right now. I'm more than I was before. Stronger.

Did you think I was tough before?

Fooled you. Some of it was just bravado. A façade.

Dealing with Drew Evans is like swimming into one of those rogue waves at the beach. He's overwhelming. And either you kick hard to keep up, or he rolls over you and leaves you behind with a face full of sand.

So I had to pretend to be a hard-ass.

I don't need to pretend anymore, because now I'm granite. Impenetrable, all the way through.

Ask anyone who's survived an earthquake at midnight, or a house fire that wipes out everything that matters. Unexpected devastation changes you.

And I mourn the old me. And my old life. The one that I had planned to share with Drew forever.

You seem confused. Sorry—let's start again.

See that woman over there? On the swing, in this empty playground?

That's me—Kate Brooks.

But not really. Not the Kate you remember, anyway. Like I said, I'm different now.

You're probably wondering why I'm here, back in Greenville, Ohio, all alone.

Technically speaking, I'm not alone.

But we'll get to that later.

The reason I'm in Greenville is simple. I couldn't bear to stay in New York. Not for another day. Not after everything.

Drew?

He's still in New York. Probably nursing a vicious hangover. Or maybe he's still drunk. Who knows? Let's not concern ourselves with him too much. He has an attractive stripper to take care of him.

Yep—I said a stripper. At least I hope she was a stripper. She could've been a prostitute.

Did you think Drew and I were going to ride off into the sunset? Live happily ever after? Join the club. Apparently happily ever after only lasts two years.

Don't check the title. You're in the right place. This is still the Drew and Kate show. It's just twisted around. Messed up. Welcome to Oz, Toto. It's a fucked-up place to be.

What's that? You think I sound like Drew? That's what Delores says—that he's infected me with his profanity. She calls it Drewspeak. I guess after two years, it kind of rubs off.

So I can see that you're wondering what happened. *You were so in love. You were so perfect for each other.* Tell me about it.

Or better yet, tell the stripper.

Anyway—believe it or not—the real problem wasn't another woman. Not at first. Drew wasn't lying when he said he'd always want me. He did. He still does.

He just doesn't want *us*.

Still don't understand? That's because I'm not telling it right. I should start at the beginning. See, last week I found out . . .

No, wait. That's not going to work either. If you're going to understand, I need to go back further.

Our end began about a month ago. I'll start there.

Five weeks earlier

"Well, hot damn, looks like we got ourselves a deal!"

The guy in the cowboy hat? Signing that stack of papers, across from me at the conference table? That's Jackson Howard Sr. The younger version in the black hat, sitting next to him? That's his son, Jack Jr.

They're cattle ranchers. Owners of the largest cattle ranch in North America, and they've just acquired the most innovative developer of GPS tracking software in the country. Now, you may ask yourself, why would two already wealthy businessmen travel across the country to expand their empire?

Because they want the best. And I'm the best.

Or should I say *we* are.

Drew takes the final document from him. "Sure do, Jack. I'd start looking into yachts for business travel, if I were you. When the profit reports roll in, your tax adviser's going to want something big to write off."

Kate and Drew.

The dream team of Evans, Reinhart and Fisher.

John Evans, Drew's father, definitely knew what he was doing when he put us together. A fact he proudly loves to remind us of.

To hear him tell it, he knew all along that Drew and I would be an unbeatable team—unless we killed each other. Apparently that was a chance John was willing to take. Of course, he didn't know we'd end up together like we are now, but . . . he takes credit for that part too. Starting to see where Drew gets it from, aren't you?

Erin walks in now with our clients' coats. She makes eye contact with Drew and taps her watch. He nods discreetly.

"I say we go out and celebrate—paint this town red! See if you city folk can keep up with the likes of me," Jackson Howard says.

Even though he's pushing seventy, he's got the energy of a twenty-year-old. And I suspect he's got more than a few bull-riding stories up his sleeve.

I open my mouth to accept the invite, but Drew cuts me off.

"We'd love to, Jack, but unfortunately Kate and I have a previously scheduled appointment. There's a car waiting for you down-stairs to take you to the finest establishments in the city. Enjoy yourselves. And of course the tab's on us."

They stand and Jack tips his hat to Drew. "That's damn fine of you, son."

"It's our pleasure."

As we walk to the door, Jack Jr. turns to me and holds out his card. "It was a real pleasure working with you, Miss Brooks. The next time you're in my neck of the woods, I'd be honored to show around. I have a feelin' Texas would agree with you. Maybe you'll even decide to stay and put down some roots."

Yep, he's coming on to me. Maybe you think that's sleazy. I would have, two years ago. But like Drew told me then, it happens all the time. Businessmen are slick, cocky. They kind of have to be.

It's one of the reasons this field has the third-highest rate of infidelity—right after truck drivers and police officers. The long hours, the frequent traveling, hooking up almost becomes inevi-table. A foregone conclusion.

It's how Drew and I started, remember?

But Jack Jr.'s not like the other jerks who've propositioned me. He seems sincere. Sweet. So I smile and reach out to take his card, just to be polite.

But Drew's hand is faster than mine. "We'd love to. We don't get a lot of work down South, but the next time we do, we'll cash in that rain check."

He's trying to be professional, unemotional. But his jaw is clenched. Sure, he's smiling, but have you ever seen *Lord of the Rings*? Gollum smiled too.

Just before he bit that guy's hand off who was holding his "pre-cious."

Drew is territorial and possessive. That's just who he is.

Matthew once told me a story: For Drew's first day of kinder-garten, his mother bought him a lunch box. A Yoda one. On the playground, Drew wouldn't put it down because it was his and he was afraid someone would break it. Or steal it. It took Matthew a week to convince him that nobody would—or that together, they could beat the everlasting hell out of anyone who did.

At times like this, I know just how that lunch box felt.

I smile kindly at Jack Jr. and he tips his hat. And then they're out the door.

As soon as it's closed behind them, Drew tears John Jr.'s card in half. "Dickhead."

I push his shoulder. "Stop it. He was nice."

Drew's eyes snap to mine. "You thought Luke and Daisy Duke's inbred love child was nice? Really?" He takes a step forward.

"As a matter of fact, yes."

His voice morphs into an over-the-top southern drawl. "Maybe I should buy myself some chaps. And a cowboy hat." Then he drops the accent. "Oohh—or better yet, we'll get *you* one. I can be your wild stallion and you can be the brazen cowgirl who rides me."

And the funniest thing of all? He's really not kidding.

I shake my head with a smile. "So what's this mysterious meet-ing we have? There's nothing on my schedule."

He smiles widely. "We have an appointment at the airport." He slides two airline tickets out of his suit pocket.

First class—to Cabo San Lucas.

I inhale quickly. "Cabo?"

His eyes sparkle. "Surprise."

I've traveled more in the last two years than I had in my entire life before—the cherry blossoms blooming in Japan, the crystal waters of Portugal. . . . All things Drew had already seen, places he'd already been to.

Places he wanted to share—with me.

I look closer at the tickets and frown. "Drew, this flight leaves in three hours. I'll never have time to pack."

He takes two bags out of the closet. "So it's a good thing that I already have."

I wrap my arms around his neck and squeeze. "You are the best boyfriend ever."

He smirks in that way that makes me want to kiss him and slap him at the same time.

"Yeah, I know."

The hotel is stunning. With views I've only seen on a postcard. We're on the top floor—penthouse. Like Richard Gere in *Pretty Woman*, Drew is a big believer in "only the best."

It's late when we get in, but after a nap on the plane, we're both wired. Energized.

And hungry.

All the airlines are cutting back these days, even in first class. The sandwiches may be complimentary, but that doesn't mean they're edible.

While Drew is in the shower, I start to unpack. Why aren't we showering together? I really don't need to answer that, do I?

I put the bags on the bed and open them. Most men look at an empty suitcase like it's some kind of physics equation—they can stare at it for hours, but still have no frigging clue what they're supposed to do with it.

But not Drew.

He's Mr. I-Think-of-Everything.

He packed all the incidentals that most men wouldn't think of. Everything I'll need to make my vacation comfortable and fun.

Except for underwear. There isn't a single pair of underwear in this entire suitcase.

And it's not an oversight.

My boyfriend happens to hold a serious grudge against undergarments. If he had his way, we'd both be walking around like Adam and Eve—minus the fig leaves, of course.

But he did bring the rest of the essentials. Deodorant, shaving cream, a razor, makeup, birth control pills, moisturizer, the rest of my antibiotic for the ear infection I had last week, eye cream—and so on.

And we should pause here, for a brief public service announcement.

I have a few clients who are in the pharmaceutical field. And those companies have whole departments whose sole job is writing.

Writing what, you ask? You know those little inserts that come with your prescription? The ones that list every possible side effect and what you should do, should any of them occur? May cause drowsiness, don't operate large machinery, contact doctor immediately, blah blah blah.

Most of us just open the little paper bag, take out our pills, and throw the insert away. Most of us do . . . but we shouldn't. I'm not going to bore you with a lecture. All I'll say at the moment is: Read the insert. You'll be glad you did.

And now—back to Mexico.

Drew walks out of the bathroom with a towel around his waist, and I forget all about the suitcase. You know how some men are boob guys, or ass guys? It works the same for women. I'm a forearm girl, myself. There's something about a man's forearms that's just . . . hot. Masculine—in a manly man kind of way.

Drew has the finest set I've ever seen. Tight and toned—not too bulky, not too thin—with just the right amount of hair.

He removes the towel from his hips and rubs it over his shoulders. And I'm pretty sure I start to drool.

Maybe I'm an ass woman after all.

"You know it's impolite to stare."

I drag my eyes up to his. He's smiling. And I take a step toward him—like a cougar closing in on her prey.

"Is it, now?"

Drew licks his lips. "Definitely." A drop of water slides down the middle of his chest.

Anyone else thirsty?

"Well, I don't want to be rude."

"God forbid."

Just as I'm about to lean down and lick the droplet off him, my stomach growls. Loudly.

Grrrrrrrr.

Drew laughs. "Maybe I should feed you first. For what I have planned, you're going to need some energy."

I bite my lip in anticipation. "You have something planned?"

"For you? Always."

He spins me around and slaps me on the rear. "Now get that delectable ass in the shower so we can go. The sooner we eat, the quicker we can come back here and fuck till the sun comes up."

He really doesn't mean to be as crude as he sounds.

Yeah—you're right—he probably does.

An hour later, we're on our way to dinner. Drew surprised me with a new dress—white eyelet and strapless, with a hem that flares out just above my knee. My hair is down with a slight curl, the way I know he loves it.

As for my boyfriend—I can't take my eyes off him. Tan slacks and a crisp white shirt, the top few buttons open, the sleeves rolled up halfway.

Gorgeous.

We arrive at the restaurant.

I've always thought the Latino culture was interesting. The music. The people. They're vibrant. Volatile.

Passionate.

All words that describe where we're dining tonight. It's dim—the only illumination comes from the candles on the tables and the twinkling lights on the ceiling. A pulsing rhythm emanates from a small band of musicians in the corner.

Drew requests in Spanish a table for two.

Yes—he speaks Spanish. And French. He's working on Japanese. Did you think his voice was sexy? Trust me—until you've heard him whisper blush-worthy phrases in a foreign language, you don't know the meaning of the word *sexy*.

We follow the robust, dark-haired hostess to a table in the corner.

Now, take a moment to look around. See all the female attention Drew gets, just by walking through the room? The appreciative glances, the inviting eyes?

I notice—I always do.

But here's the thing: Drew doesn't. Because he's not looking. At any of them.

For you guys out there who think looking doesn't hurt? You're wrong. Because we women don't think you're just enjoying the view. We think you're comparing, finding us lacking. And that stings. Like a paper cut on your eyeball.

I'm fully aware that Drew could have any woman he wants—the model in Beverly Hills, the heiress on Park Avenue. But he picked me. He fought for me. So when we go out, it's a major boost to my confidence.

Because I'm the only woman he's looking at.

We sit at the table and scan the menus. "So explain to me again how you made it through college and business school without ever drinking straight tequila?"

I laugh at the question, remembering. "Well, back in high school, we'd have these bonfires—campouts."

You ever sleep with an empty two-liter soda bottle for a pillow? It's not fun.

"So one night, Billy and the guys were drinking tequila—and Billy swallowed the worm. And then he started to hallucinate. We were working on amphibian anatomy in bio at the time, and as messed up as he was, Billy was convinced he was a frog—and that Delores was trying to dissect him. He hopped off into the woods by himself, and it took us three hours to find him—with his tongue in the dirt. I've been hesitant to try tequila ever since."

Drew shakes his head. "Confirming, once again, what I've known all along. Billy Warren is, and always has been, a complete fucking idiot."

I'm used to Drew's digs against Billy. And in this case? He's not exactly wrong.

So I tell him, "As long as you don't to make me swallow the worm, I'll give it a go."

His eyes light up, like a kid in a bike shop. "You know what this means?"

"What?"

He wiggles his brows. "I get to teach you how to do body shots."

⁓

Although I don't believe you need to be drunk to have great sex, having a good buzz certainly doesn't hurt.

Drew and I are in the elevator heading back to our room, both of us more than tipsy from the tequila. I can taste it on Drew's tongue—bitter with a touch of citrus. He has me pinned against the wall, my skirt bunched up around my hips, and we're pushing and grinding against each other.

I'm glad there's no one else in the elevator—although at this point? I'm really too far gone to give a damn.

We stumble into the room.

Still groping and kissing.

Drew slams the door and spins me around. In one quick movement he pulls the dress down my body, leaving me bare. Except for my heels.

I lean over the desk, resting on my elbows. I hear the hiss of a zipper—and then I feel him. Sliding his cock between my lips—testing the waters—making sure I'm ready.

I'm always ready for him.

"Don't tease," I whimper.

Between the tequila and the elevator, I'm really turned on. Needy. He pushes in slowly but to the hilt. And I sigh.

Now, we all know the old phrase that bigger is better. And Drew is big—not that I have a lot to compare him to, but he's twice the size of Billy.

I'm not making you boys out there uncomfortable, am I? News flash—this is how woman talk. At least when you're not around to listen.

Anyway, it's not really size that makes the man. It's rhythm—the pace—knowing how to hit all those delicious spots with just the right amount of pressure. So the next time you see an infomercial for Cockgrow or Miracle-Dick?

Save your money. Buy the Kama Sutra instead.

Drew grabs my hair, pulling my head back, and moves quicker. Hard and fast. I grip the edge of the desk, holding on for balance.

He kisses my shoulder and whispers in my ear, "You like that, baby?"

I moan. "Yes . . . yes . . . so much."

He thrusts into me with more force, shaking the desk.

And just like that, I'm coming like an out-of-control locomotive.

I'm floating. Weightless.

And it's sublime.

Drew slows the movement of his hips as I come down, drawing it out—making it last. He pulls me back against his chest and his fingers skate up across my stomach and up to my breasts, cupping and kneading them with both hands.

I raise my arms around his neck, turning my head, bringing his mouth to mine.

I love his mouth, his lips, his tongue. Kissing is an art form, and Drew Evans is Michelangelo.

He pulls out of me and I turn around to face him. Backing him up to the bed. Drew sits on the edge and I climb on, wrapping my legs around his waist.

God, yes.

This is how I like it best—chest to chest, mouth to mouth, not an inch of space between us. I take him in my hand and slide down onto him. My insides stretch with the fullness and Drew moans. I rise slowly and slam down hard. Testing the strength of the bed springs.

Squeak.

Squeak.

I move faster. Deeper. Our bodies are slick from the Mexican heat.

And then Drew is holding my face in his hands, his thumbs moving back and forth across my skin. Suddenly tender. Worshipful.

Our foreheads press together and in the dim light I can see his eyes looking down, watching where he moves in and out of me.

And I look down too.

It's erotic. Sensual.

I push his hair back from his forehead.

And my voice is begging, "Tell me you love me."

He doesn't say it often. He prefers to show me. But I never get tired of hearing it. Because every time he actually says the words, I'm filled with same wonderment as the first time.

"I love you, Kate."

His hands still hold my face. Both of us panting—moving faster—getting closer. It feels spiritual.

A holy communion.

Drew's voice is hushed. Breathless. "Tell me you'll never leave me."

His eyes are soft now, liquid silver. Pleading for reassurance.

For all his audacity and overconfidence, I think there's a part of him that's still haunted by the week he thought I'd chosen Billy over him. I think that's why he works so hard to prove how much he wants me.

To show me that I chose wisely.

I smile softly and look right into his eyes.

"Never. I'll never leave you, Drew."

The words feel like vows.

His hands grip my hips, raising me up, helping me move.

"God, Kate . . ." His eyes close.

And our mouths open, giving and taking each other's breaths. He expands inside me, throbbing, as I clamp down hard around him.

And we come together. In perfect unison.

Perfect splendor.

Afterward, Drew's arms tighten around me. I touch his face and kiss him gently. He falls backward on the bed, taking me with him, keeping me on top. We lie like that for a while until our heart rates come back down and our breathing slows.

And then Drew rolls me under him.

And we do it again.

Chapter 2

The New York City club scene.

Pounding music that only allows for conversation if you're a lip-reader. Sweaty guidos in their I'm-too-sexy silk shirts, who think breathing is a sign that you're interested. Impossibly long lines at the bar and insanely priced watered-down drinks.

Not really my favorite place to be.

I'm more of a bar girl. Bottled beer, jukeboxes, pool tables—I can be quite the pool shark when I need to be.

Not that I haven't enjoyed a good rave or two in my time.

What? You thought pot was the only illegal substance to grace my bloodstream? Afraid not. Ecstasy, acid, 'shrooms—I've tried them all.

You look a little shocked. You shouldn't be.

The whole drug culture was started by intellectuals in institutions of higher learning. Don't even try and tell me Bill Gates came up with Windows—a maze of interconnected, multicolored pathways—without some serious psychedelic assistance.

Anyway, despite my preferences, four weeks after Cabo, Drew and I end up at the hottest club of the moment. With our best friends, Matthew and Delores. To celebrate their first anniversary.

You didn't know they got married? It was great. Vegas. Need I say more?

Delores is into dance clubs. She enjoys any kind of sensory stimulation. When we were ten, her mother, Amelia, bought her a strobe light for her bedroom. Delores would sit and stare at it for hours, like it was a crystal ball or a Jackson Pollock painting.

Now that I think about that, it explains a lot.

Anyway, see us there? Delores and Matthew are just walking off the dance floor, to where I'm sitting in a circle of trendy over-stuffed red chairs. Drew went to get another round.

I'm just too damn tired to dance tonight. Delores falls into the chair next to me, laughing.

I yawn.

"You look like shit, Petunia."

A good friend should be able to tell you anything. Maybe your boyfriend's screwing around, or a dress makes your love handles hang over like a shar-pei's skin? In either case, if they're not brave enough to tell it like it is? They're not your best friend.

"Thanks, Dee Dee. Love you too."

She flips her long blond hair back, crimped and shining with glitter for this evening's festivities. "I'm just saying, you look like you could use a spa day."

She's not wrong. I've been exhausted all week—that full-body type of weariness that feels like you're carrying weights on your ankles and your ribs. Yesterday, I actually fell asleep at my desk.

Maybe I'm coming down with the flu that's going around.

Delores fans herself with her hand. "Where the hell is Drew with those drinks? I'm dying here."

He's been gone a few minutes, which isn't unusual in a place like this.

Still, my eyes scan the room.

And then they find him. By the bar, drinks in hand, talking to a woman.

A beautiful blond woman with legs as long as my whole body.

She's wearing silver stilettos and a sequined minidress. She looks . . . fun. You know the type—one of those cool girls who guys love to hang out with because they burp and watch sports. She's smiling.

More important, Drew is smiling back.

And do you see the way she's leaning toward him? The tilt of her head? The subtle rubbing of her thighs?

They've had sex. No doubt about it.

Son of a bitch.

This isn't the first time I've been faced with one of Drew's past random hookups. In fact, it's pretty much an everyday occurrence—the waitress at Nobu, the bartender at McCarthy's Bar and Grill, several random patrons at Starbucks. Drew is polite but brisk, paying them no more attention than an old classmate from high school whose name you can't quite remember.

So it doesn't normally bother me.

But like I said, this isn't a normal week. Fatigue has made me short-tempered. Overly sensitive. Pissed off.

And he's still fucking talking to her.

She puts her hand on his arm, and my inner cavewoman pounds her chest like King Kong in drag. There's an empty glass in front of me. Remember Marcia Brady and the football? Think I could reach them from here?

Have you ever noticed that serial killers and mass murderers are almost always male? That's because men like to spread agony around. Females, however, turn our pain inward. Keep it to our-selves. Let it fester.

Yes, I took Psych 101 in college.

But the point is, instead of going over there and ripping out Blondie's hair extensions like I want to, I stand up.

"I'm going home."

Delores blinks. "What? Why?" Then she sees my face. "What the hell did that moron do now?"

Some advice—when you're angry with your significant other, try not to tell your friends. Because after you've forgiven him? They'll never forget.

I recommend complaining to his family instead. They've already seen all his negative, selfish, immature traits in full swing—so it's not like you're letting the cat out of the bag.

I shake my head, "Nothing. I'm just . . . tired."

She doesn't buy it. And her gaze locks on to where I'm still looking. Legs throws her head back and laughs. Her teeth are pearly white and perfect. Apparently the bulimia hasn't rotted the enamel away.

Yet.

Delores turns to her husband. "Matthew, go collect your friend. Before I go over, because then you'll need a mop to collect him."

I raise my chin stubbornly, "No, Matthew—don't. Drew is obviously happy right where he is. Why drag him away?"

Immature? Possibly.

Do I care? Nope.

Matthew looks back and forth between us. Then he rushes off in Drew's direction.

Dee Dee has him so well trained. She puts the Dog Whisperer to shame.

I hug her good-bye. "I'll call you tomorrow."

And then I head for the door without looking back.

⁓⁓

I've never lived by myself.

At eighteen, I went from my parents' house to a dorm room. Sophomore year, Billy joined Delores and me in Pennsylvania, and we leased a huge dilapidated house off campus with four other students. The roof leaked and the heat sucked, but the rent was right.

After Delores left for New York, while I was still at Wharton, Billy and I got a place of our own. Then we moved to the city too—and you know the rest.

Why am I telling you this?

Because I'm not as independent as I come off. I'm one of *those* women. The kind who turns on every light in the house when she's home by herself. The kind who sleeps over at a friend's when her boyfriend's out of town.

I've never been alone. Never not had a boyfriend. It's one of the reasons Billy and I lasted so long—because I preferred an expired relationship to none at all.

When I get back to the apartment, I head to the bedroom and change into a tank top and cherry-colored pajama pants. As I finish washing the makeup off my face, I hear the front door open and close.

"Kate?"

I don't answer.

His footsteps come down the hall, and a moment later Drew

fills the bathroom doorway. "Hey. Why'd you leave? I came back with the drinks and Delores starts chucking ice cubes at my head, calling me a shit heel."

I don't make eye contact. And my voice is stiff. Dismissive. "I was tired."

Why don't I just tell him what's bothering me? Because this is the game women play. We want you to drag it out of us. To show us you're interested. It's a test—to see how much you care.

Drew follows me into the bedroom. "Why didn't you wait for me? I would've come with you."

I raise my eyes to his. My face is tight, my body tense, ready for battle. "You were otherwise occupied."

He looks down, eyes squinting. Trying to decode my words.

Then he gives up.

"What are you talking about?"

I spell it out for him.

"The blonde, Drew. At the bar?"

He regards me with curiosity. "What about her?"

"You tell me. Did you fuck her?"

Drew scoffs. "Of course I didn't fuck her. I left two minutes after you did. We both know I last a hell of a lot longer than that. Or do you need a reminder?"

No, he's not as obtuse as he seems. It's kind of brilliant, actually. He's trying to be cute. Sexy. Trying to distract me.

It's what he does. And usually it works. But not tonight.

"Have you *ever* fucked her?"

Drew rubs the back of his neck. "You really want me to answer that?"

That's a big fat yes, in case you were wondering.

I throw my hands up. "Of course! Of course you screwed her—because God forbid we go one *day* without seeing someone that your dick isn't intimately acquainted with! Not that you even remember them half the time."

Drew's eyes narrow. "So which is it? Are you pissed off when I do remember them, or when I don't? Throw me a clue here, Kate, so I can give you the fight you're obviously hell-bent on having."

I pick up my body lotion and rub it swiftly over my arms. "I don't want to fight—I just want to know why you remember her."

Drew shrugs, and his tone turns neutral. "She's a model. Her billboard's in the middle of Times Square. It's a little hard to forget someone when you see her picture every day."

And doesn't *that* just make me feel *so much* better.

"How nice for you. Why are you even here then? Why don't you go back and find your little model, if she means so much to you?"

A small part of me realizes I'm being irrational, but my anger is like a mudslide—now that it's started, there's just no way to hold it back.

Drew looks at me like I've gone crazy and holds out his hand. "She doesn't mean anything to me. You know that. Where the fuck is this coming from?"

And then a thought occurs to him.

He takes a step back before asking, "Are you due for your period? Don't freak out—I'm only asking because, the way you've been acting lately, I think Alexandra's title is in jeopardy."

He could have a point. In high school, there was this hallway, the L wing, that was always really crowded between classes. And I knew my period was coming when I'd walk down that hallway and want to jab my pencil into the neck of the person in front of me.

However—for you guys out there? Even if your girlfriend's

tirade *is* PMS derived? Don't point that out to her. It won't end well for you.

I pick up my shoe and throw it, hitting Drew right between his bright blue eyes.

His hands go to his forehead. "What the shit?! I told you not to freak out!"

Every relationship has a screamer. A thrower. A breaker of things. In this one, that would be me. But it's not my fault. You can't blame the nuclear missile for going off after all its buttons have been pushed.

I pick up the other shoe and throw that one too. Drew grabs a pillow and uses it as a shield. I retreat to the closet for more ammo, but he grabs my arm before I can get there.

"Would you fucking stop! Why are you being like this?"

I glare up at him. "Because you don't even care! I'm really upset here—and you don't give a shit!"

His eyes open wide, incredulous.

"Of course I give a shit—I'm the one getting Jimmy Choos thrown at my head like Chinese freaking stars!"

"If you care so much, why don't you apologize?!"

"Because I didn't fucking *do* anything! I have no problem crawling on my hands and knees when I screw up. But if you think I'm gonna beg because you've been possessed by the Hormone Demon, you're out of your mind, sweetheart."

I break out of his hold and push him on the chest with both hands. "Fine. That's fine, Drew. I don't care what you do anymore." I grab a blanket and pillow and shove them at him. "But you're sure as shit not sleeping next to me after you do it. Get out!"

He looks down at the linens. Then back at me. And his face relaxes, turning calm.

Too calm—like the kind before a storm.

"I'm not going anywhere."

He throws himself on the bed, spreading his arms and legs wide like a kid making a snow angel.

"I happen to like this bed. It's comfy. Cozy. I've made some great memories here. And this is the *only* place I'm sleeping."

There's no point in arguing when Drew gets like this—willful and childish. Sometimes I actually expect him to hold his breath until he gets his way.

I whip the pillow out from under his head, leaving him flat on the mattress, looking up at me.

His brow furrows. "What are you doing?"

I shrug. "I said I'm not sleeping with you. So if you won't take the couch, I will."

He sits up. "This is frigging insane, Kate—tell me you realize that. We're fighting over nothing!"

My voice rises. "So now my feelings mean *nothing*?"

"I didn't fucking say that!"

I point a finger at him. "You said we're fighting over nothing, and we're fighting about how you made me feel—so that means you think my feelings are nothing!"

His mouth opens, like a fish searching for oxygen.

"You lost me. I have no idea what you just said."

I close my eyes. And just like that, my anger deflates.

Hurt fills me instead.

"Forget it, Drew."

As I walk down the hall, his voice follows me.

"What the fuck just happened?"

I'm too tired to try and explain it anymore. Usually when we argue, I have a hard time falling asleep. I'm too charged up with adrenaline, with passion.

But that's not a problem tonight. I'm out like a narcoleptic as soon as my head hits the pillow.

Sometime later—could be three minutes or three hours—a warm, hard chest presses against my back, waking me up. I feel his hand on my stomach. He presses his face into my hair and inhales.

"I'm sorry."

See, boys, that's all you have to do. Those really are the magic words—capable of overcoming any obstacle.

Even PMS.

I turn in his arms, and look into his eyes. "What are you sorry for?"

Drew's face goes blank, searching for the correct answer. Then he smirks. "Anything you want me to be sorry for."

I laugh, but my words are sincere. "No. I'm sorry. You were right—I was just being a bitch. You didn't do anything wrong. I'm definitely premenstrual."

He kisses my forehead. "It's not your fault. I totally blame Eve."

I kiss his lips softly. And then his neck. I trail a path across his chest, moving around his pecs, suddenly awake with the urge to please him. I look up at him. "You want me to make it up to you?"

His fingers trace what I'm sure are dark circles under my eyes.

"You're exhausted. How about you make it up to me in the morning?"

I pull myself closer and rest my cheek against his skin. I close my eyes, ready to go back to sleep.

Until Drew's voice breaks the silence.

"Unless . . . you know . . . you really *want* to make it up to me now. Because if you do, far be it from me to—"

I laugh out loud, cutting off his words as I duck my head under the covers, slowly traveling downward to make it up to him.

In his most favorite way.

Chapter 3

Two days later, we're having breakfast at the kitchen table. Drew likes to exercise in the evening after work, to decompress and release the stress of the day. I, however, am one of those highly annoying people who love to go for a five a.m. run. Breakfast is where we meet in the middle. After which, Drew goes to the office and I shower.

"You know what I love about Cookie Crisp cereal?" He's staring at his spoon.

I've never seen one person ingest so much cereal. I swear, if I didn't cook, it's all he would eat.

I swallow a mouthful of yogurt—Dannon Light & Fit. The commercials don't lie; it's really delicious. Strawberry banana is the best.

"What's that?"

"It's shaped like cookies. So, not only is it awesome, but I feel like I'm getting revenge on my parents for making me eat frigging oatmeal the first half of my life."

A poet and a philosopher, Drew is truly a Renaissance man.

I open my mouth to tease him, but I snap it shut as a wave of nausea strikes like a lightning bolt. I clear my throat and bring the back of my hand to my lips.

"Kate? You okay?"

As I try to answer, my stomach does a somersault that would make Nadia Comăneci jealous.

I'm going to throw up.

I hate throwing up.

It makes me feel claustrophobic. Suffocated.

To this day, when I have a stomach virus, I sit on the phone with my mommy while she talks me through the heaves.

I'm not going to make it to the bathroom, so I lunge for the kitchen sink. As I splatter my breakfast into it, Drew holds back the strands of hair that have escaped my ponytail.

I want to tell him to go away, but another round of retching commences. Some women have no problem going to the bathroom, passing gas, or throwing up in front of their boyfriends.

I'm not one of them.

Maybe it's stupid, but if I were to die suddenly, I don't want the last image Drew has of me to be one where I'm sitting on the toilet.

Or in this case, barfing in the sink.

His voice is kind. Soothing. "Okay . . . easy. You're okay."

When it seems like the worst is over, Drew hands me a wet paper towel. Then he glances toward the drain. "Well, that's colorful."

I croak, "Ugh—I knew I was getting the flu."

"Seems like it."

I shake my head. "I don't have time be sick. I have the Robinson meeting today." Anne Robinson is a client I've been courting for months. Old money—and I stress the word *old*. She's like, ninety-five. If I don't sign her today, it might literally be too late to sign her at all.

"You're sick, baby. And I don't think Mrs. Robinson will be impressed if you yak all over her antique brooch. Lucky for you, you have a genius boyfriend who performs exceedingly well in clutch situations. Give me the folder—I'll run the meeting. Annie's as good as yours."

He scoops me up in his arms.

"Drew, no—"

He cuts me off. "Nope. No bitching. Don't want to hear it. I'm putting you to bed."

I smile weakly.

Drew tucks me in and leaves a glass of ginger ale on the nightstand.

I think he kisses my forehead, but I can't be sure. Because I'm already drifting off to sleep.

❦

Three hours later, I walk out of the elevator onto the 40th floor of our office building.

My stomach's empty, but after a good nap, I woke up feeling better. Refreshed. Ready to take on the world and Anne Robinson. I walk to the small conference room and peer through the glass.

Can you see Drew? Sitting next to the little gray-haired lady in the wheelchair? While he's speaking to the legal representation seated around the table, Mrs. Robinson's hands disappear under it.

And a second later Drew flinches, like he's been given an electric shock.

Old women have a thing for Drew.

It's completely hilarious.

He gives Mrs. Robinson a harsh look. She just wiggles her eyebrows. Then he rolls his eyes before looking away, spotting me in the process.

Drew excuses himself and comes out into the hall, relief shining on his face like a beacon. "For the love of all that is holy—thank God you're here."

My lips slide into a smirk. "I don't know; Mrs. Robinson seems to be enjoying your company."

"Yeah—if she tries enjoying it any more, I'm going to staple her hands to the conference table."

Then he looks me over, concerned. "Don't think I'm not over-fucking-joyed to see you, 'cause I am. But what are you doing here? You're supposed to be in bed."

I shrug. "Must've been a three-hour bug. I feel fine now."

Drew cups my cheek and palms my forehead, feeling for a fever. "You sure?"

"Yep. Right as rain."

He nods, but his eyes are suspicious, not totally convinced. "All right. Oh—we're supposed to have dinner at my parents' tonight. Think you'll be up for it, or do you want me to cancel?"

Dinner at the Evanses' is always an interesting affair.

"I should be good to go."

He hands me the Robinson folder. "Okay. Your investment strategies got them all quivery. They're wet and spread-eagled, just waiting for you to nail them."

His imagery is slightly disturbing.

"That's gross, Drew."

He's unperturbed. "You say tomato, I say tomahto." Then he kisses me quickly. "Go get 'em, killer."

He walks away and I head into the conference room to seal the deal.

So you're starting to get it now, aren't you? The problem, the big picture? I know it's taking a while, but we're getting there.

Enjoy the good times while you can—they won't be lasting much longer.

The reason I'm showing you all this, is so you'll understand why I was so shocked. How accidental—unintended—it all really was.

I guess life is like that.

You think you have it all under control. Your path so perfectly mapped out. And then one day you're driving along and *bam!* You get rammed from behind on the freeway.

And you never saw it coming.

People are like that too. Unpredictable.

No matter how well you think you know somebody? How confident you are of their feelings, their reactions? They can still surprise you.

And in the most devastating of ways.

Chapter 4

Visiting with Drew's family is never boring. Coming from a single-child home, I found the family gatherings a little overwhelming at first. But now I'm used to it.

Drew and I arrive last.

Frank Fisher—Matthew's father—and John Evans stand by the wet bar in the corner, trading stock quotes. Delores is perched on the arm of the recliner beside Matthew, watching the football game, while Drew's sister, Alexandra, aka "The Bitch," and her husband, Steven, sit on the couch.

Mackenzie, Drew's niece, sits on the floor. She's changed since the last time you saw her. She's six years old now, her hair is longer, her face a little thinner—more girlish, less toddler, but still adorable. She's playing with a gaggle of dolls and miniature nursery accessories.

Drew's mother, Anne, and Matthew's mom, Estelle, are most likely in the kitchen. And if you're wondering where Steven's widowed father, George Reinhart, is, we won't be seeing him until later.

As we walk into the room, Steven greets us and offers us both a drink.

We settle on the love seat, drinks in hand, and watch the game.

Mackenzie pushes a button on one of her dolls, and an animatronic voice fills the room. "No, no, no! No, no, no!"

Mackenzie's head tilts as she looks at the annoying doll. "I think you're wrong, Daddy. No-No Nancy doesn't sound like Momma at all."

The comment gets Alexandra's attention. "What do you mean, Mackenzie?"

Behind his wife's shoulder, Steven shakes his head at his daughter, but unfortunately for him, she doesn't get the message.

Instead she explains, "The other day, when you were out, Daddy said No-No Nancy sounds just like you. But instead of no, you say, 'Nag, nag, nag.'" All heads turn to Alexandra, watching her like a ticking time bomb counting down to zero.

Steven tries valiantly to defuse her. He smiles and teases, "You have to admit, honey, the resemblance is uncanny. . . ."

Alexandra punches him in the arm. But he tightens his bicep before she makes contact, absorbing the blow. She punches him again, less playfully.

Steven just boasts, "You can't dent steel, babe. Be careful— don't want to hurt your hand on the gun."

Faster than a speeding bullet, Alexandra's fingers lash out and pinch the tender flesh on the back of his tricep, bringing him to his knees.

Drew grimaces and rubs the back of his own arm in sympathy. "That's gonna leave a mark."

Alexandra's voice is firm. And final. "I don't nag. I'm a kind, nurturing, supportive wife, and if you would just do what you're supposed to, I'd never have to say anything at all!"

He yelps, "Yes, dear."

She releases his arm and stands. "I'm going to help my mother in the kitchen."

After she leaves, Mackenzie looks down at the chastising doll thoughtfully, then up at her father. "Actually, you're right, Daddy. Momma really does sound like Nancy."

Steven puts his finger to his lips. "Shhhh."

A while later, Drew, Matthew, Delores, and I are in the den for Mackenzie's guitar lesson.

I'm teaching her to play. I was five when my father taught me. He told me music was like a secret code, a magical language that would always be there for me. To comfort me when I was sad, to help me celebrate when I was happy.

And he was right.

It's a lesson I've treasured my entire life. A small piece of him that I was able to hold on to after he was gone. And I'm thrilled to be able to pass that knowledge on to Mackenzie.

She's playing "Twinkle, Twinkle, Little Star" right now.

She's good, isn't she? Focused. Determined. I'm not surprised—she's Drew's niece, after all. As she finishes the song, we all clap.

Then I turn to Delores. "Billy called me last night. He's got a few weeks off. He's coming to the city next week and wants to meet up for dinner."

Sarcasm drips off Drew's words like chocolate on a strawberry. "Jackass is coming to town? Oh, goody. It'll be like Christmas."

Delores looks at Drew. "Hey—Jackass is my nickname for him. Get your own."

Drew nods. "You're right. Douche Bag has a much nicer ring to it."

Are you wondering about the Bad Word Jar? For those of you who don't know, the Bad Word Jar was started by Alexandra to financially penalize anyone—usually Drew—who cursed in front of her daughter. Originally, each curse cost a dollar, but when Drew and I were working through our issues, I convinced Mackenzie to bump the price up to ten. Color me vindictive.

Anyway, these days, the Jar is no longer used. Mackenzie has a checking account now. And since she's old enough to write, she keeps a log of who owes what in that blue notebook there—the one she's scribbling in right now.

We're all expected to pay our fines before we leave. Or run the risk of a 10 percent late fee.

I have a feeling Mackenzie's going to be a brilliant banker someday.

She puts her book down and goes back to strumming her guitar. Then she turns to Drew.

"Uncle Drew?"

"Yes, sweetheart?"

"Where do babies come from?"

Drew doesn't even hesitate. "God."

I got the basics when I was eleven. My mother took the "stay my little girl forever and don't ever have sex" approach. Amelia Warren, on the other hand, was more than willing to fill in the gaps. She wanted her daughter Delores and me informed. And prepared. By the time we were thirteen, we could get a condom on a banana faster than any hooker on the strip.

Whatever you do, don't let your kids learn about procreation from "The Video." Finding out about the birds and the bees is a lot like finding out there's no Santa—kids are bound to figure it out eventually, but it'll go down much easier coming from you.

Mackenzie nods and goes back to her guitar. Until . . .

"Uncle Drew?"

"Yes, Mackenzie?"

"The baby grows in the mommy's tummy, right?"

"More or less."

"How does that happen . . . exactly?"

Drew rubs his fingers over his lips, thinking it over.

And I hold my breath.

"Well, you know when you're painting? And you mix blue and red together? And you get . . ."

"Purple!"

"Excellent, yes, you get purple. Babies are kind of like that. A little blue paint from the daddy, some red paint from the mommy, shake it all together, and boom—you get a whole new person. Hopefully not purple, but if Aunt Delores is involved? Anything is possible."

Delores gives Drew the finger behind Mackenzie's back.

Mackenzie nods. And goes back to strumming her guitar. For one whole minute.

"Uncle Drew?"

"Yep?"

"How does the daddy's blue paint get to the mommy's red paint?"

Drew raises both eyebrows. "How . . . how does it . . . get there?"

Mackenzie gestures with her hand. "Well, yeah. Does the doctor give her a shot of blue paint? Does the mommy swallow the blue paint?"

Matthew snickers. "Only if the daddy is a very lucky guy."

Delores smacks him on the head. But Mackenzie's round blue eyes stay on Drew, waiting for an answer.

He opens his mouth.

And then closes it.

He starts again.

And then stops.

Finally, like cannonballing into a pool on the first day of spring, he takes the plunge. "Well . . . the mommy and daddy have sex."

It's official. Alexandra's going to kill him. For real this time. I'm going to be a widow before I'm ever a wife.

Mackenzie's face rumples with confusion. "What's sex?"

"Sex is how babies get made."

She thinks about it a moment. And then she nods. "Oh. Okay."

Wow.

And I thought the final exams in business school were hard.

Drew handled that pretty well, don't you think? He's good with kids. Which makes sense, because in so many ways . . . he still is one.

Alexandra walks into the room. She seems happy, now—now that she's showed Steven that his "steel guns" can, in fact, be dented. She's all glowy.

"What are we doing in here?"

Drew smiles innocently. "Talking about paint colors."

Alexandra smiles and strokes her daughter's hair.

As Mackenzie adds, "And sex."

Alexandra's hand stops. "Wait . . . what?"

Drew leans over and whispers in my ear, "We should probably leave the room now."

As the door swings closed behind us, we hear "Drew!" And Alexandra doesn't sound so happy anymore.

At last, dinner is served. The actual eating of the meal is uneventful, but during dessert Alexandra taps her glass with a spoon.

"Everyone—can I have your attention, please?" She beams at Steven and then goes on. "Mackenzie has an announcement she'd like to make."

Mackenzie stands on her chair and proclaims, "My mom and dad had sex!"

The entire table is silent.

Until Matthew raises his glass. "Congratulations, Steven. It's like Halley's Comet, right? You only get to come every seventy-five years?"

Delores laughs.

And John clears his throat. Awkwardly. "That's, ah . . . that's . . . very nice, dear."

Then Frank decides to share. "Sex is good. Keeps you regular. I make sure I have sex at least three times a week. Not that my Estelle is into any of that freaky-freaky stuff, but in forty years of marriage, she's never had a headache."

Estelle smiles proudly beside him.

And Matthew covers his face with his hands.

The rest of us just stare. Eyes wide, mouths slightly opened.

Until Drew throws his head back and laughs. "That's so great." He wipes his eyes, practically crying.

Alexandra shakes her head. "Wait. There's more. Go ahead, Mackenzie."

Mackenzie rolls her eyes. "Well, that means they're gonna have a baby, of course. I'm gonna be a big sister!"

Congratulations erupt all around. Anne tears up as she hugs her daughter. "I'm so happy for you, honey."

Drew stands and hugs his sister sweetly. "Congratulations, Lex." Then he smacks Steven on the back. "I'll keep the guest room ready for you, man."

I'm confused. "Guest room?"

Drew explains. "The last time Alexandra was pregnant, she kicked Steven out—not once, not twice, but *four* fucking times."

Matthew joins in. "And that's not counting the time she let him stay, but she threw all his shit out the window."

Drew chuckles. "It looked like a Barneys delivery truck exploded on Park Avenue. The homeless were never dressed so well."

Alexandra rolls her eyes and turns to me. "Pregnancy hormones. They can cause some pretty bad mood swings. I tend to get a little . . . bitchy . . . when I'm pregnant."

Drew smirks. "As opposed to the rest of the time, when you're just so pleasant?"

You know how some dogs still keep chewing your shoes—no matter how many times you smack them with a newspaper? They just can't resist?

Drew is one of those dogs.

Alexandra turns on her brother like a cat hissing at a snake. "You know, Drew, being with child? It's kind of like a 'get out of jail free' card. There's not a jury in the country that would convict me."

He backs away slowly.

I shake my head at him, then ask Alexandra, "Other than that, how are you feeling?"

She shrugs. "Tired, mostly. And the vomiting doesn't help. Most women get morning sickness, but I get it at night, which sucks pretty bad."

Huh

Vomiting.

Tired.

Moody.

They certainly sound familiar.

What? Why are you looking at me like that?

No, no—everyone knows the surest sign of pregnancy is a missed period. And my period's not due for . . . one . . . two . . . four . . .

Five . . .

My period was due five days ago.

Oh.

My.

God.

Chapter 5

Denial is a skill I mastered at a young age.

Don't think about it. Don't talk about it. Suck it up. Choke it down.

I didn't cry the night my father died.

Not when Sherriff Mitchell came to our door to take us to the hospital, or when the doctor told us they'd lost him. I didn't shed a tear during the wake—or at the funeral.

Thank you for your condolences.

Yes, I'll be strong for my mother.

You're so kind.

Eight days after he was laid in the ground, my mother was working in the diner downstairs. I was in our kitchen, trying to open a jar of pickles.

I walked into my parents' bedroom and called my Dad for help. And that's when it hit me—staring at their empty room. He wasn't there. He'd never be there again. I collapsed on the floor and sobbed like a baby.

Over a jar of pickles.

It's that same skill set that gets me through the rest of the night at the Evanses'. I smile. I chat. I hug Mackenzie good-bye. Drew and I go home and make love.

And I don't tell him.

You don't yell fire in a movie theater unless you're sure there're flames.

Have you ever seen *Gone with the Wind*? Scarlett O'Hara is my idol.

"I can't think about this now. I'll think about it tomorrow."

So that's my plan. At least for the moment.

Tomorrow comes quickly.

And apparently God has a sick sense of humor. Because everywhere I turn, I'm surrounded by pregnancy.

Take a look:

The dog walker passing me on the sidewalk, the police woman directing traffic, the man on the cover of *People* magazine at the newsstand, the fellow executive in the cramped elevator who looks like she's smuggling a contraband medicine ball under her blouse.

I cover my mouth and keep my distance, like a tourist trying to avoid the swine flu.

Eventually, I make it to my office. I sit at my desk and open my trusty daily planner.

Yes, I still use a paper-based calendar. Drew bought me a BlackBerry for Christmas, but it's still in the box. I don't trust any device capable of banishing my work to the unknown abyss with the touch of a button

I like paper. It's solid—real. To destroy it, you have to burn it.

Usually I'm pretty anal retentive. I write *everything* down. I'm a banker—we live and die by the schedule. But lately I've been distracted; preoccupied by exhaustion and the overall feeling of crappiness. So I missed the fact that I'd started a new pack of birth control pills, but never got a period for the last one.

And speaking of birth control pills—what's up with that?

Ninety-nine-point-nine percent effective, my ass.

It's the same statistical accuracy of those pee-on-a-stick pregnancy tests—so I'm not going near one of those. Instead, I pick up the phone and call the office of Dr. Roberta Chang.

Remember those four other students who Delores, Billy, and I lived with off campus in Pennsylvania? Bobbie was one of them. Her husband, Daniel, was another.

Bobbie's an amazing person. Her parents emigrated from Korea when she was just a baby. She's petite—tiny enough to shop at GAP Kids—but she's got the personality of an Amazon.

She's also a brilliant ob/gyn. That would be a baby doctor for you guys out there.

Bob and her husband moved to New York just a few months ago. I haven't seen her in years, but ours is one of those friendships that can go a decade without contact; then when we finally do get together, it's like we haven't missed a day.

I make an appointment and automatically mark it in my planner.

Bob—7:00.

I close the book and place it next to the phone on my desk. Then I glance at the clock and realize I'm late for a meeting.

Shit.

I grab a folder and head out the door.

Still not thinking about it . . . in case you were wondering.

When I get back two hours later, Drew is sitting at my desk, tapping a pen impatiently against the dark wood. We usually eat lunch together—order in—and share it in one of our offices.

"Hey."

He glances up. "Hi."

"Did you already order, or were you waiting for me?"

He looks confused. "Huh?"

I perch myself on the edge of the desk. "Lunch, Drew. That's why you're here, right?"

He shakes his head. "Actually, I wanted to check in with you about dinner. A new place opened in Little Italy, and I could really go for some pasta. I was going to make reservations for us tonight. At seven."

I freeze.

I don't have a lot of practice with lying. Not since high school, anyway. Even then, there weren't a lot of outright lies. More . . . omissions of activities my mother would have blown a gasket over. When it was necessary to lie, Delores was my go-to girl, my alibi. That hasn't changed.

"I can't tonight. Delores wants to have a girl's night. We haven't had one of those in a while."

Let's pause for a moment. This is important.

Can you see his face? Look closely or you'll miss it.

For just a second, there's a flash of surprise. A touch of anger . . . maybe hurt. But then he catches himself, and his expression smooths back out to neutral. I missed that look the first time around. You should remember it. It'll make a lot more sense in about ten hours.

Drew's voice is flat. Like a detective trying to trip up a perpetrator. "You just saw Delores last night."

My stomach gurgles like Pop Rocks in soda. "That was different—everyone was there. Tonight it'll just be the two of us. We'll grab a few drinks, eat some fattening appetizers, and then I'll come home."

Drew stands, his movements hurried, tense. "Fine, Kate. Do whatever the fuck you want."

He tries to walk past me, but I grab onto his belt. "Hey. Don't be like that. We can go out to dinner tomorrow night. Don't be mad."

He lets me pull him closer, but he doesn't say anything. I give him a flirty smile. "Come on, Drew. Let's do lunch. And then afterward, you can do me."

I rub my hand up his chest, trying to soften him up.

But he doesn't give. "I can't. I have some work to finish. I'll talk to you later. "

He kisses my forehead, and his lips seem to linger a moment longer than normal. Then he pulls back and walks away.

In New York City, there's one thing you can depend on. Expect. It's not the mail, or the kindness of your fellow man.

It's rush-hour traffic. Never fails. It's what I'm sitting in right now.

Bumper to bumper.

I tried calling Delores three times to fill her in on my covert operation, but she didn't answer. Cell phones aren't allowed in the lab. I also haven't seen Drew since he walked out of my office, and that's a good thing. I really don't want to talk to him until I know what I'm dealing with.

When you're alone in a practically unmoving vehicle, there's really not much to do.

Except think.

Can you guess what I'm thinking about? Even the strongest dam is going to crack eventually.

Scarlett O'Hara has left the building.

Did you ever hear the story about Delores's father? It's a doozy.

When we were young, Amelia told Delores that her daddy just couldn't live with them. She kept it simple—kind. But when she was older, Delores got the full story.

Amelia grew up in California. Can't you just picture it? Amelia the surfer chick—young and tan, lean and laid-back.

When she was seventeen, she met a guy at the Santa Monica Pier—dark hair, chiseled arms, and eyes the color of jade. His name was Joey Martino. They had an instant "connection," and like Juliet before her, Amelia fell fast and hard.

Then it came time for Joey to move on, and he asked Amelia to come with him. Her mother told her if she walked out the door, she wouldn't be allowed to walk back in.

Ever.

Amelia hugged her little sister good-bye and hopped on the

back of Joey's Harley. About six weeks later, they were passing through Greenville, Ohio.

And Amelia realized she was pregnant.

Joey took the news well, and Amelia was thrilled. Now they'd be a real family.

But the next morning, all she woke up next to was a note. It read:

> *It was fun.*
> *Sorry.*

Amelia never saw him again.

Some kids need to get burned a few times before they stop playing with matches. But Amelia was never that kind of kid. One lesson was all she needed. From then on, she only dated a certain type of man—humble, simple—not smooth or flashy or arrogant. Guys who were nothing like Joey.

Who were nothing like Drew.

It's why she doesn't like him.

No—that's not quite right. It's why Amelia doesn't trust him.

She took me aside that first Christmas, when she and my mother came up to visit. She told me to go slow, to watch myself with Drew.

Because she'd seen his kind before.

Anyway—story time's over, kids.

We're here.

Bob's office is nice—a homey-looking brownstone with a real, live parking lot. Those are hard to come by in the city, in case you didn't know. It's a busy lot, shared with the building next door. Cars come and go and jockey for spaces.

I kill the engine and grip the steering wheel. And take a deep breath.

I can do this.

I mean, really—it's only the next eighteen years of my life, right?

I get out of the car and stare at the small sign in the window of the building.

ROBERTA CHANG
GYNECOLOGY AND OBSTETRICS

As I try to get my feet to move, two large hands come from behind me and cover my eyes. A familiar voice whispers in my ear, "Guess who?"

I turn around, bursting at the seams. Living with someone, particularly during the college years, creates a bond born of shared experiences and precious memories.

"Daniel!"

Daniel Walker is a mammoth-sized guy. He and Arnold Schwarzenegger could totally be brothers. But don't let that fool you. He's like one of those Werther's candies—hard on the outside, soft and gooey on the inside.

He's affectionate. Giving. Compassionate.

During our junior year, a mouse decided to move into our ramshackle house. All of us voted to kill it—except Daniel. He constructed a trap with string, cardboard, and a stick that would have made the Little Rascals proud.

And he actually caught the little bugger. We kept him. In a cage, kind of like a mascot. We named him Bud after our favorite beer.

Daniel pulls me into a bear hug, picks me up, and spins me around. Then he sets me on my feet and kisses my cheek. "It's so good to see you, Kate. You look great!"

I'm smiling so hard, my face hurts. "Thanks, Daniel. You too. You haven't changed a bit. How's everything going?"

"Can't complain. Things are good—busy. I'm still interviewing at hospitals."

Daniel's an anesthesiologist. Whenever they can, he and Bob work together. Like me and Drew.

He goes on. "But Bobbie's practice is booming, so I'm the gofer boy for now." He holds up a bag of Chinese takeout.

When the smell hits my stomach, it twists, letting me know it is not pleased. I swallow hard.

He throws a heavy arm over my shoulders and we chat for a several minutes. About their move, about Delores and Billy. I tell him about Drew and how I want the four of us to get together for dinner.

And then there's a loud screech of rubber tires.

We both turn and watch the taillights of a speeding car disappear out of the parking lot.

Daniel shakes his head. "And I thought Philadelphia drivers were bad."

I chuckle. "Oh, no—New Yorkers have the monopoly on bad driving. And crazy baseball fans. Don't wear your Phillies jersey here; it could end in bloodshed."

Daniel laughs and we head into the building.

Well, it's official.

Life as I know it is over.

I'm pregnant. Knocked up. The bun is in the oven and that bad boy is baking. I wasn't really surprised. Just hoping I was wrong.

According to Bobbie, my antibiotics were the culprit. They lower the effectiveness of birth control pills.

So you see what I was saying about those pamphlets? Read 'em. Learn 'em. Live 'em.

It's too soon to do an ultrasound, so I have to come back in two weeks. And every day I also have to take prenatal vitamins that are big enough to choke a large elephant.

Lucky me.

I park my car in the garage, but I don't go up to the apartment. One of the best parts of living in the city is that there's always someplace that's open, somewhere to walk to with people around.

I head out onto the sidewalk and walk a few blocks, trying to clear my head. Trying to figure out what the hell I'm supposed to do now.

If you're wondering why I don't sound happy, it's because I'm not. You have to understand—I was never *that* girl. I didn't play with baby dolls; I played with my parents' cash register. When the other kids wanted to go to Toys "R" Us, I wanted to go to Staples.

Even before my craving for financial independence began, my dreams revolved around office buildings and desks—not cradles and baby carriages. It's not that I don't want children. I just don't want one *now*. Now was not part of the plan.

And then there's Drew. He loves me, I know. But pregnancy changes things. It means stretch marks and saggy boobs and sleepless nights. No more spontaneous vacations. No more sex marathons.

He's going to freak out. Definitely.

I sit down on a bench and watch the cars drive by.

Then a voice to my right grabs my attention.

"Who's a good boy? Andrew is! My sweet boy."

It's a woman with soft blond curls and dark eyes, about my age. And she's holding a doe-headed bundle of drool.

Do you believe in signs? I don't.

But my grandmother did. She was an incredible woman—a respected archaeologist who did extensive study on the southern Native American tribes. I worshipped my grandma. She once told me that signs were all around us. Guides to point us in the right direction, toward our fate. Our destiny. That all we had to do was open our eyes and our hearts, and we would find our way.

So I watch the young mother and her child. And then a man comes up to them.

"Hey. Sorry I'm late. Damn meeting ran over."

I assume he's her husband. He kisses her. Then he takes the bundle from her and holds it up over his head.

"There's my guy. Hey, buddy."

And his smile is so warm, so beautiful, it literally takes my breath away. The golden couple lean against each other tenderly, the baby between them, pulling them together like a magnet.

I feel like a voyeur, but the moment is so precious I can't look away.

And that's when it hits me. I'm not just pregnant. I'm having a *baby*. Drew and I made a *baby*. A whole new person.

And an image appears in my head. So clear. So perfect.

A dark-haired little boy, with Drew's smart-ass smile and my sparkling personality. A part of each of us.

The best parts.

I think about the way Steven looked at Alexandra last night when they announced the big news. I picture the way Drew watches me when he thinks I'm not looking. And the way he cuddled with Mackenzie when she fell asleep beside him on the couch. I remember how wonderful it feels to teach her to play the guitar.

And how amazing it would be to teach a baby . . . everything. Drew would adore having a small someone to show things to—like how to play chess, and basketball.

And how to curse in four different languages.

Drew isn't Joey Martino. His family means everything to him. *I* mean everything to him.

And I'm having his baby. *Oh my God.* The pregnancy hormones must be on overload, because tears fill my eyes and stream down my cheeks. Happy tears.

Because it's going to be okay.

Maybe I will have stretch marks, but this is New York—the plastic surgery capital of the world. And sure, there are things I want to accomplish professionally. And I will. Because Drew will be there to help me. To support me. Like he has since the day I met him.

He's going to be excited—like a kid getting an unexpected gift on Christmas morning. It'll be a shock at first, but can't you just see him? Elated. Overjoyed.

"Excuse me, miss, are you all right?" I must be crying louder than I thought, because Baby-Daddy is looking at me with concern.

I wipe at my cheeks, embarrassed. "Yes, I'm fine. I'm just . . ." I gaze at their child. "He's just so beautiful. You're all so beautiful."

I break down in a round of fresh sobs, and the mother takes a step back.

Great. Now I'm the crazy lady on a bench.

She asks, "Is there someone you need us to call?"

I take a breath and pull myself together. And then I smile. "No. I'm all right. Really. It's just . . . I'm having a baby."

There.

I said it.

Sure, I just said it to two perfect strangers, which is a little messed up, but still. Am I scared? Of course I am. But I've never run from a challenge in my life—why would I start now?

"Well, congratulations, and good luck to you, miss."

"Thank you."

The family turns and walks down the street together. As I watch them go, a store display to the right catches my eye. It's a Yankee merchandise store, and in the window is a teeny-tiny T-shirt that says, FUTURE YANKEES PITCHER. And my excitement blooms like a flower in a rainforest.

Because now I know just how I'm going to tell Drew.

Chapter 6

What do you know about ESP? Extrasensory Perception; the knowledge of an incident before it takes place. We all have a little bit of it—that other ninety percent of our brains we don't use.

It's those times in the car when you think of a song you haven't heard in years, and it's the next one that comes on the radio. It's those mornings when you picture an old friend and at dinnertime the phone rings, and it's the friend you were thinking of.

I was never a big believer in that sort of thing. But as the store clerk handed me my change for the tiny T-shirt, a ball of anxiety settled deep in my gut.

And it wasn't normal butterflies. It was urgent. Desperate unease, like when you realize you forgot to pay a credit card bill.

I had to get to Drew. I had to talk to him—to tell him—and it had to be now. I walked quickly down the street. Well . . . as quickly as I could in three-inch heels.

As every step carried me closer to our building, the worry increased exponentially.

At the time I chalked it up to the news I was about to break. But looking back now, I think it was something else.

Precognition.

By the time I stood outside our apartment door, my knees were shaking and my palms were sweaty. Then I reached for the knob. . . .

If you have a weak stomach? You may not want to watch this.

It won't be pretty.

⁓⁓

I step into the apartment. The lights are out. I put my keys on the table and take off my coat. I flick the switch on the wall, flooding the room with light.

And that's when I see him.

Them.

Drew is standing in the middle of our living room, his dress shirt unbuttoned, exposing the chest that I've traced my fingers over a thousand times. The warm, bronze skin I love to touch. He has a half-empty bottle of Jack Daniel's in one hand. And the other hand is hidden. Buried.

In a mane of wavy auburn hair.

She's the opposite of me in every way. Thick red tresses, breasts the size of watermelons, perky in their fakeness. She's tall—as tall as Drew—even without the stilettos. Her lips are red and lush, plump enough to make Angelina Jolie envious.

And those plump red lips are moving against Drew's mouth.

Good kissers, really good kissers, don't just use their lips. They utilize their entire body—their tongue, their hands, their hips.

Drew is a good kisser.

But I've never had the chance to observe him in action. I've never seen him kiss anyone. Because I've always been on the receiving end. The kissee.

But that's not the case now.

I stand there—stunned. Watching. And though it's only for a few seconds, it feels like forever. Like an eternity.

In hell.

Then Drew pulls back. And almost as if he knew I was here all along, his eyes find mine immediately. They're hard. Merciless.

And his voice is as cold as the steel of an outdoor gate in a snowstorm.

"Look who's home."

Lots of women imagine how they would react if they caught their boyfriend or husband cheating. What they would say. How strong they'd be.

Righteous and indignant.

But when it's for real? When it's not just pretend predictions? Those emotions are peculiarly absent.

I'm numb inside.

Dead.

And my voice is nothing more than a whispered stutter.

"What . . . what are you doing?"

Drew shrugs. "Just having a little fun. I figured, why should you be the only one who gets to?"

I hear the words, but I don't understand them. My eyes squint and my head tilts, like a bewildered dog.

Drew steps away from the redhead and takes a swig from the bottle. He flinches as he swallows.

"You look confused, Kate. I'll explain. The first rule of lying is always get the alibi straight. See—right now, Matthew and Delores are on a plane to Vegas. Matthew's been planning the trip for weeks—a surprise second honeymoon. So I knew you were full of shit this afternoon. I just needed to see if you'd actually go through with it. So I followed you. Gotta love the GPS."

Last year, a woman named Kasey Dunkin disappeared after a night out with friends in the city. It was all over the news. The police were able to trace her cell to an abandoned warehouse in Brooklyn, and even though she'd been stabbed multiple times, she survived. Drew and I had the same kind of program installed on our phones the next day.

"You followed me?"

He followed me to Bob's office. He knows where I went. Does that mean . . .

"Yep. I know where you were. I know everything. I fucking saw you."

He knows. . . . Drew knows I'm pregnant.

And obviously he's not pleased.

My voice rises as I speak, gaining momentum. "You know?" I point at the woman who's watching us like we're her own personal soap opera. "And *this* is how you react?"

Drew looks confused. "Do you frigging even know me at all? How the fuck did you think I'd react?"

I've seen Drew annoyed before.

Thoughtless.

Frustrated.

But this is different.

This is . . . cruel.

He asks me, "You're not even gonna try and deny it? Make me think I'm delusional?" For a moment his face crumples. And he looks . . . anguished—like a torture victim about to break his silence. "Aren't you going to tell me I'm wrong, Kate?"

He blinks and the anguished look is gone. And I'm pretty sure I just imagined it.

Wishful thinking.

I fold my arms across my chest. "I won't discuss this with you in front of an audience."

Drew's jaw locks stubbornly. "Are you going to end it?"

My feet move back away from him, all on their own.

And my hand drops protectively to my abdomen.

"What?"

He repeats himself, impatient with my shock. "I said—are you going to fucking end it?"

Politically, Drew is pro-choice. Despite his Catholic upbringing, he respects and loves the women in his family far too much to let some old man on Capitol Hill dictate what they can or can't do with their bodies.

But emotionally—morally—I've always thought he was pro-life. So the fact that he's standing here telling me to abort a child, *our child,* is just . . . incomprehensible.

"I haven't . . . I haven't had time to think about it."

He laughs bitterly. "Well, you better start thinking, because until your little indiscretion is out of the picture? I don't even want to fucking look at you—let alone discuss *anything.*"

His words hit me like a gust of wind on a cold day. The kind that leaves you breathless.

Drew isn't Joey Martino.

He's worse.

Because he wants me to choose. An ultimatum. Like he did with Billy.

And what the hell is he talking about—*my* indiscretion? Like I made it happen all by myself?

And then it sinks in—his anger. His vindictiveness. It starts to make sense.

"Do you think I *planned* this? That I did it on purpose?"

He smirks, and even a deaf person would be able to hear the sarcasm. "No—of course not. These things *just happen* sometimes, right? Even when you don't mean them to."

I open my mouth to argue, to explain, but the stripper's giggle cuts me off. I glare at her. "Get out of my house before I put you out with the rest of the trash."

In situations like this? Women can cut each other down faster than a tree dealer on Christmas Eve. But it's not because we're petty. Or catty.

It's because it's easier to go after a nameless woman than to admit that the true fault lies with the man who was supposed to love you. Who was supposed to be committed. Faithful.

And wasn't.

She says, "Sorry, honey, you're not paying for this show. I go where the money man tells me."

Drew loops an arm around her waist and smiles proudly. "She's not going anywhere. We're just getting started."

I find the strength to raise a brow. And try to land a shot of my own.

"Paying for it now, Drew? Isn't that pathetic."

He smirks. "Don't kid yourself, sweetheart—I've been paying for it for the last two years too. You've just been slightly more expensive than the average whore."

I should have known better. Arguing with Drew is like dealing with a terrorist. He has no boundaries; nothing's off limits. There are no depths he won't sink to to win.

Then he looks thoughtful.

"Although I must say, despite how everything's turned out, you were money well spent. Especially that night, against the kitchen sink"—he winks—"worth every penny."

I'm dying. Each horrible word cuts into me like a blade slicing skin. Can you see the blood? Oozing slowly with every atrocious syllable. Drawing it out, making it more painful than it ever needed to be.

You look surprised. You shouldn't be.

Drew Evans doesn't burn bridges. He sets dynamite to them. Decimating the bridge, the mountains it connects, and any other living thing unlucky enough to be within a fifty-mile radius.

Drew never does anything halfway. Why should destroying me be any different?

I turn to walk down the hall before I crumble in front of him like an Egyptian pyramid.

But he grabs my arm. "Where are you going, Kate? Stick around—maybe you can learn a new trick."

You know how someone's personality can make him more attractive? Like that kid in high school who, despite the lack of muscle tone and the case of mild acne, was able to run with the popular crowd? Because he told the funniest jokes and had the best stories.

I wish I could tell you it worked in reverse. I wish I could say that Drew's words magically transformed his face into the monstrosity he sounds like.

But I can't.

Look at him.

I imagine this is what Lucifer looked like when God tossed him out of heaven. Bitter and broken.

But still so achingly beautiful.

I pull my arm free. And my voice is high-pitched, almost hysterical. "Don't touch me! Don't you ever fucking touch me again!"

He smiles slowly, the very picture of serenity. He wipes his hand on his pants, like he just handled something dirty.

"That really won't be a problem for me."

I'm going to be sick. I'm going to throw up all over his black Bruno Magli shoes.

And it's got nothing to do with the pregnancy.

I go down the hall, forcing myself to walk. Because I refuse to let Drew see me run from him.

I barely make it to the bathroom in time.

I drop to my knees and hold on to the toilet for dear life. A nail breaks and my knuckles turn white. My stomach contracts and I heave violently. Blood pounds in my ears and acid burns my throat.

I cough and I sob, but my eyes are dry. There are no tears.

Not yet. That part comes later.

How can he do this? He told me he wouldn't . . . and I trusted him. When he said he loved me. When he promised he'd never hurt me.

I believed him.

We never talked about having kids. We never talked about *not* having them either. But if I had known he'd be this way, I would have been more careful. I would have . . .

God.

Listen to me. My boyfriend is in the living room with another woman on his lap, and I'm sitting here thinking of all the things *I* could have done to keep it from happening?

And I called *Drew* pathetic.

When there's nothing left in my stomach, I pull myself up to the sink and look in the mirror. Splotchy cheeks and dull red-rimmed eyes stare back at me from a face I don't recognize.

I douse my face with cold water, over and over. Drew may have ripped me apart—turned me into a quivering mass of shame and self-recrimination—but it'll be a cold day in hell before I let him see that.

I stumble to the bedroom, grab a duffel bag out of the closet, and blindly fill it with the first things my hands touch. I have to get away. From him. From everything that reminds me of him.

I know what you're thinking. *"Your career, everything you've worked for—you're throwing it all away."*

And you're right—I am. But none of that matters anymore. It's like . . . like those poor people who jumped from the towers on September eleventh. They knew it wouldn't save them, but the fire was too hot and they had to do something, *anything,* to get away from the pain.

I zip the bag shut and put it on my shoulder. Then I brace my hand against the door and I breathe. Once. Twice. Three times. I can do this. I just have to make it to the door. It's only a dozen steps away.

I walk down the hall.

Drew is sitting on the couch, legs spread, eyes on the dancing woman swaying in front of him, the bottle of Jack beside him. I focus on his face. And for just a moment, I let myself remember.

Grieve.

I see his smile—that first night in the bar—so boyishly charming. I feel his lips, his touch, the first night we made love, here, in this apartment. All heat and need. I relive every tender word, every loving moment since then.

And I lock it all away.

In a box of steel, banished to the farthest corner of my mind. To be opened later. When I'm able to fall apart.

I step into the room and stop just a few feet from the couch. Redhead dances on, but I don't look at her. My eyes never leave Drew's face.

My voice is raw. Scratchy. But surprisingly resolute.

"I'm done. With you, with all of this. Don't track me down a week from now and tell me you're sorry. Do not call me and say you've changed your mind. We. Are. Over. And I never want to see you again."

How many parents have told their teenagers that they're grounded forever? How many teenagers have responded that they'll never speak to them again?

Over. Forever. Never.

Such big words. So final.

So hollow.

We don't really mean them. They're just things you say when you're looking for a reaction. Begging for a response. The truth is, if Drew came to me tomorrow or next month, or six months from now, and told me he'd made a mistake? That he wanted me back?

I'd take him back in a heartbeat.

So do you see now what I was saying before? I'm not a strong woman.

I'm just really good at acting like one.

Drew's voice is blunt. "Sounds good." He toasts me with the bottle. "Have a rotten fucking life, Kate. And lock the door on your way out—I don't want any more interruptions."

I want to tell you he hesitated. That there was a hint of regret on his face or a shadow of sadness in his eyes. I would stay if there was.

But his face is blank. Lifeless—like a dark-haired Ken doll.

And I want to scream. I want to shake him and slap him and smash things. I want to, but I don't. Because if you try and hit a brick wall? All you'll get is a broken hand.

So I pick up my bag and lift my chin. And then I walk out the door.

Chapter 7

The defining characteristic of a Type-A personality is having goals and having the strategies to achieve those goals. I'm most definitely a Type A.

Planning is my religion; the To-Do List is my bible.

But as I reach the middle of the lobby of the building that has been my home for the last two years, I freeze. Because for the first time in my life, I have no idea what to do next. No direction.

And it's terrifying. It feels weightless—like an astronaut cut from his anchor, drifting out into space. Desolate. Doomed.

My life revolves around Drew. And I never thought I'd need a contingency plan.

My hands start to shake first, then my arms, my knees. My heartbeat spikes and I'm pretty sure I'm hyperventilating.

It's the adrenaline. The fight-or-flight response is an amazing phenomenon. It's action without thought—movement without permission from the brain.

And mine is in full swing. Every limb screams at me to move. To *go*. My body doesn't care where, as long as it's not here. *Run, run as fast as you can, you can't catch me, I'm the Gingerbread Man.*

The gingerbread man was lucky. He had someone chasing him.

"Miss Brooks?"

I don't hear him at first. The sound of my own panic is too deafening—like a thousand bats in a sealed cave.

Then he touches my arm, grounding me, bringing me back down to earth. "Miss Brooks?"

The gray-haired gentleman with the concerned green eyes and dashing black cap?

That's Lou, our doorman.

He's a nice guy—married twenty-three years, with two daughters in college. Have you ever noticed that doormen are always named Lou, or Harry, or Sam? Like their name somehow predetermined their occupation?

"Can I get you anything?"

Can he get me anything?

A lobotomy would come in handy right about now. Nothing fancy—just an ice pick and a hammer, and I'll be a happy member of the spotless mind club.

"Are you all right, Miss Brooks?"

You know that saying, "It's better to have loved and lost than never to have loved at all?"

That's a crock. Whoever said it didn't know a fucking thing about love. Ignorance is better; it's painless.

But to know perfection—to touch it, taste it, breathe it in every day—and then have it taken away? Loss is agony. And every inch of my skin aches with it.

"I need . . . I have to go."

Yes, that was my voice. The dazed and confused version, like a casualty in some massive car wreck, who keeps telling anyone who'll listen that the light was green.

It wasn't supposed to end like this. It wasn't supposed to end at all. He wrote it in the clouds for me, remember?

Forever.

Lou glances at the bag on my shoulder. "You mean to the airport? Are you late for a flight?"

His words echo in the bottomless pit that is now my mind. *Airport . . . airport . . . airport . . . flight . . . flight . . . flight.*

When Alzheimer's patients start to lose their memories, it's the newest ones that go first. The old ones—the address of the house they grew up in, their second-grade teacher's name—those stick around, because they're ingrained. So much a part of the person that the information is almost instinctual, like knowing how to swallow.

My instincts take over now. And I start to plan.

"Yes . . . yes, I need to get to the airport."

You know anything about wolves? They're pack animals. Familial.

Except when they're injured.

If that happens, the wounded wolf sneaks off in the night alone, so as not to attract predators. And it goes back to the last cave the group occupied. Because it's familiar. Safe. And it stays there to recover.

Or die.

"Lou?" He turns toward me from the doorway. "I need some paper and a pen. I have to send a letter. Could you mail it for me?"

New York City doormen don't just open doors. They're deliverymen, mailmen, bodyguards, and gofers.

"Of course, Miss Brooks."

He hands me a clean sheet of paper and a high-end ballpoint pen. Then he goes outside to hail my cab. I sit down on the bench and write quickly. Any nine-year-old can tell you that's the best way to rip off a Band-Aid.

Kind of feels like a suicide note. In a way, I guess it is.

For my career.

Mr. John Evans:

Due to unforeseen personal circumstances, I will no longer be able to fulfill the terms of my contract with Evans, Reinhart and Fisher. I hereby submit my resignation without notice.

Regretfully,

Katherine Brooks

It's cold, I know. But professionalism is the only shield I have left.

You know, for a girl, there's something special about a father's approval. Maybe it's some evolutionary leftover from the times when daughters were just property, to be bartered and sold to the highest bidder. Whatever the reason, a father's endorsement is important—it carries more weight.

When I was ten, the Greenville Parks and Recreation Department had Little League tryouts. Without a son to pour his baseball dreams into, my dad spent his time teaching me the finer points of the game. I was a tomboy anyway, so it wasn't hard.

And that year, my father thought I was too good to play softball with the girls. That the boy's league would be more of a challenge.

And I believed it. Because *he* believed it.

Because he believed in me.

Billy made fun of me; he said I was going to get my nose

broken. Delores came to watch and paint her nails on the bleachers. I made the team. And when the season ended, I had the best pitching record in the whole league. My dad was so proud, he put my trophy next to the cash register at the diner and bragged to anyone who wanted to listen. And even to those who didn't.

Three years later, he was gone.

And it was crippling because, like a blind person who at one time could see, I knew exactly what I was missing. I never played baseball again.

Then later, I met John Evans. He picked me—chose me—out of a thousand applicants. He nurtured my career. He was proud of every deal I closed, every success.

And for just a moment, I knew how it felt to have a father again.

And John brought me to Drew. And our lives intertwined, like ivy around a tree. You know how it is—his family became my family, and all that comes with it. Anne's gentle admonishments, Alexandra's protectiveness, Steven's jokes, Matthew's teasing . . . sweet Mackenzie.

And now I've lost all them too.

Because although I don't think they'll agree with what Drew has done, how he's treated me, you know the saying: Blood is thicker than water. So in the end, no matter how distasteful they find Drew's choices, they won't be siding with me.

"Miss Brooks, your car's outside. Are you ready?"

Before I fold the letter, I scribble two words under my signature. Two painfully inadequate words.

I'm sorry.

Then I force my legs to stand, and I hand Lou the addressed envelope. I walk toward the door.

From behind me, the elevator chimes. And I stop and turn to the big gold double doors.

I wait.

Hope.

Because this is how it always happens in the movies, isn't it? *Some Kind of Wonderful, Pretty in Pink,* and every other John Hughes film I grew up watching. Just before the girl walks away or gets in the car, the guy comes sprinting down the street.

Chasing after her.

Calling her name.

Telling her he didn't mean it. Not any of it.

And then they kiss. And the music plays and the credits roll.

That's what I want right now. The happy ending that everyone knew was coming.

So I hold my breath. And the doors open.

You want to guess who's in there? Go ahead—I'll wait.

.
.
.
.
.
.
.
.
.
.
.
.
.
.
.
.
.

.

.

.

It's empty.

And I feel my chest cave in on itself. My breaths come quick, panting through the pain—like when you twist an ankle. And my vision blurs as the elevator doors slowly close.

It seems so symbolic.

I guess I've got my own doors to close now, huh?

I wipe my eyes. And sniff. And I adjust the bag on my shoulder.

"Yeah, Lou. I'm ready now."

Chapter 8

A sshole.

They say grief is a process. With stages.

Bastard.

And breakups are a lot like a death. The demise of the person you were, of the life you'd planned to have.

Cocksucker.

The first stage is shock. Numbness. Like one of those trees in a forest—after a fire has ripped through it—that are scorched and hollow, but somehow still standing.

Like someone forgot to tell them you're supposed to lay down when you're dead.

Dick toucher.

Care to hazard a guess what the second stage is?

Oh yeah—it's anger.

What have you done for me lately—I'm better off without you; I never liked you anyway—anger.

Ear-fucker. No, that's lame. *Eater-of-ass.*

Better.

The alphabetical naughty name-calling? It's a game Delores and I made up in college. To vent our frustration against the out-of-touch, stick-up-the-ass professors who were giving us a hard time.

Feel free to jump in anytime. It's cathartic.

And for some reason, a lot easier when you're a high college student.

Fuckface.

Anyway—what was I saying? That's right—anger.

Gooch.

Fury is good. Fire is fuel. Steam is power. And rage keeps you standing, when all you really want to do is curl up in a ball on the floor like a frightened armadillo.

Herniated Intestine.

Here's a fact for you: Married men live seven to ten years longer than bachelors. Married women, on the other hand, die about eight years earlier than their single counterparts.

Are you shocked? Me neither.

Infected dick cheese.

Because men are parasites. The life-sucking variety from the rainforest that burrow up your genitalia, then lay eggs in your kidneys.

And Drew Evans is their leader.

Jerk-off.

The flight attendant asks me if I would like a complimentary beverage.

I'm on the plane. Did I not mention that?

I don't take the drink; I'm trying to avoid the airplane bathroom. Too many memories there. Fun, sweet memories.

Kooch.

See—Drew doesn't like to fly. He never came out and said it, never let it stop him, but I could tell.

Flying requires you to hand someone else the reins—to let go of the illusion of control. And we all know Drew has enough control issues to fill the Grand Canyon.

Right before takeoff, he'd get moody. Tense. And then, after the seat belt sign went off, he'd suggest a joint trip to the lavatory. To relieve some of that tension.

I could never say no.

The Mile High Club? I'm a gold member now.

Leaky discharge.

After the cart moves past me, I recline my seat back and close my eyes. And I think about what every scorned woman dreams of.

Payback.

Suffering.

Punishment.

Molester of Llamas.

Not that I'm going to go all Lorena Bobbitt on him. A woman's most powerful weapon is guilt—much more lethal than a machete. So my revenge scenarios revolve around . . . death.

My death.

Sometimes it's cancer; sometimes it's childbirth. But in every one, Drew is banging on my deathbed door, begging to come in, to tell me how assholishly wrong he was.

How sorry he is.

But he's always too late. I'm already gone. And that knowledge destroys him—leaves him wrecked. Ruined.

The guilt eats at him slowly, like a tooth in a glass of Coca-Cola.

Nutsack puller.

And he spends the rest of his life alone wearing black, like an eighty-year-old Italian grandma.

Orca fingerer.

I smile.

It's such a nice thought.

Pillow-biting pansy.

That's a double-word score.

Delores would be so proud.

Queef.

Oh, yeah—I went there.

Rim job.

You know, I think it's better this way. No bullshit. If I look at the situation objectively, I'm better off this way.

Drew did me a favor.

Smegma eater.

Because even though he likes to play dress-up in Daddy's big-boy suits? Emotionally, he's an adolescent. A child.

Testicle licker.

The kind no one else likes to play with. Because when a game's not going his way? He smashes the board to pieces.

Urinary tract infection.

And who needs that?

Not me. No, sir. I deserve more.

Vagina.

I'm going to get through this. I'm Kate Fucking Brooks.

I will succeed.

I will survive.

I will persevere.

Whoreboy.

Even if it's just to spite him. Stubborn is my middle name.

X-tra absorbent maxipad.

I was fine before Drew, and I'll be fine after him.

Just because I've never been alone doesn't mean I can't be.

I. Don't. Need. Him.

Really.

Yeasty seepage.

Are you convinced?

Zithead.

Yeah.

Me neither.

I know what you're thinking. *Why?* That's the big question, isn't it? The one Nancy Kerrigan made famous. The one everyone wants answered when tragedy strikes.

Why, why, why?

Human beings like explanations. We crave reasons, something to blame. The levees were too low, the driver was drunk, her skirt was too short—the list is endless.

The drive from Akron to Greenville takes about three hours. That's a lot of time to drive. And think. And I spent the whole trip thinking about *why*.

If I had it to do all over again, I would have asked him. I wish I could say it was all some terrible mistake. A misunderstanding— like in *Romeo and Juliet* or *West Side Story*.

But really, what are the chances of that? If I had to guess, I'd say Drew just wasn't ready to grow up—to take on that level of responsibility. Of commitment.

Look at my hand. Do you see a ring? That's not an accident.

He's a wonderful uncle to Mackenzie. Dedicated. Nurturing. The kind of man who would beat the hell out of another shopper for the last Tickle Me Elmo or Cabbage Patch Kids doll, two days before Christmas. He'd do anything for her.

But being a father is different. It's all *on* you and yet nothing is ever *about* you again. And that's the part I think Drew couldn't handle.

Personally, I blame Anne and Alexandra. Don't get me wrong, they're good people, but . . . let me put it this way: Last summer, Alexandra had us all up to her parents' country place for Mackenzie's birthday. Drew and I got there late because we pulled over on a deserted road to make out.

By the way—car sex? It's a wonderful thing. If you ever want to feel young and uninhibited, do it in the backseat. But I digress.

So there we are, hanging out by the pool, and I get up to grab a slice of pizza. But does Drew get up? Of course not. Because his mother has already heated him a crispy, fresh slice in the kitchen. And his sister brought it right to his lounge chair—with a cold beer.

Were his legs broken? Was he suffering from some early onset Parkinson's disease that made it impossible for him to heat up his own food? Or—God forbid—eat it cold? No. That's just the way they are with him, the way they've always been.

Coddling. Overindulgent.

And I can't help but think that if Anne and Alexandra had let him get his own goddamn pizza once in a while, then maybe he would have taken the news better. Been more prepared.

In the end, it doesn't really matter. Knowing why doesn't change anything. So as I passed the WELCOME TO GREENVILLE sign, I promised myself that I wouldn't ever ask why again. I wouldn't waste the energy.

But you know something? God has a sick sense of humor.

Because I would be asking why *again* in just a few short days.

For a completely different and infinitely more devastating reason.
Sorry to be the one to tell you this, but yes—it does actually get
worse.

You'll see.

Have you ever visited your high school years after you graduated?
And the desks and the windows and the walls are the same . . . yet
it still looks different? Smaller somehow.

That's what this feels like.

Driving down Main Street, coming home, it's all exactly like
I remember it . . . but not. The red awning outside Mr. Reynold's
hardware store is green now. Falcone Pharmacy turned into a Rite
Aid. But the gaudy pink palm tree is still in the window of Penny's
Beauty Salon where Delores and I got our nails done before prom.
The old green park bench is still there, too, outside my parents'
restaurant, where I used to chain my bike after school.

I park the car and get out, my duffel bag hanging on my shoulder. It's a little after noon, and the sun is high and hot, and air
smells like sand and burning tar. I cross the street and open the
door. The hum of conversation simmers down as I stand at the
entrance, and a dozen friendly, familiar faces look me over.

Most of the people in this room have known me since I was
born. To them, I'm Nate and Carol's daughter—the small-town,
dark-haired, pigtailed girl who made good. Who beat the financial
odds and did her family proud. I'm the success story the grade
school teachers tell their students about, in the hopes of inspiring
them to bigger dreams than the automobile factory has to offer.

I force my lips to smile politely, nodding and waving brief greetings as I make my way between the tables, toward the door in the back. See the sign?

EMPLOYEES ONLY.

I blow out a big breath. And all the anger that kept me going—that got me here—goes out with it. Exhaustion swamps me. And I feel drained, empty. My limbs are boneless, like I just crossed the finish line of a ten-mile uphill marathon.

I push the door open. And the first thing I see is my mother, bent over a table, scanning a produce delivery list.

Beautiful, isn't she? I know most daughters think their mothers are pretty—but mine really is. Her dark brown hair is pulled into a high ponytail, like mine. Her skin is fair and clear, with the barest of lines around her lips and eyes. If wrinkles are hereditary, I've hit the genetic jackpot.

But beyond her looks, my mother's beautiful on the inside. It sounds clichéd, but it's true. She's unchanging. Steady. Dependable. Life hasn't always been easy for her—or kind. But she moved forward, carried on, with dignity and grace. My mother isn't an optimist. She's stoic, like a statue that's still standing after a hurricane.

The door swings closed behind me and she lifts her head. Her eyes light up and she smiles big. "Kate!" She puts the list down and moves toward me.

Then she sees my face. And the corners of her smile fall like a feather in the wind. Her voice is hushed and laced with concern. "Kate, what's wrong?"

My arms give up, and my bag drops to the floor.

She takes another step.

"Katie? Honey? What happened?"

Now, there is an excellent question. I should answer—but I

can't. Because my hands are covering my face. And the only sounds that escape my lips are gasping sobs.

Her arms pull me forward, strong and warm and smelling of Downy April Freshness. And she holds me, tight and secure, like only a mother can.

Remember the steel box? Yeah, it's open now. And everything that happened comes spilling out of it.

Chapter 9

The average human being spends a third of their life in bed. Eight thousand, three hundred, thirty-three days. Two hundred thousand hours.

Why am I telling you this? Because you should never feel bad about spending a lot of money on decent bed linens. A good blanket is priceless. When you're young, it protects you from the boogeyman. And when you're not so young, it keeps your old bones warm.

My mother pulls my down comforter up to my chin, tucking me into my childhood bed, like a six-year-old during a thunderstorm.

After my meltdown in the break room, she brought me upstairs to the small but quaint two-bedroom apartment above the diner where I was raised. Where my mother still lives. The home of my youth.

She wipes at the tears that stream down my cheeks. I hiccup and stutter, "I-I-I'm . . . s-so . . . s-s-stupid."

I was valedictorian of my high school class. I graduated from Wharton Business School.

Ignorance is not something I'm familiar with. So I can't help but feel that I should have known—should've seen this coming.

After all, I lived with Drew for two years. How long does it take for a leopard to change its spots?

Oh, that's right—they don't.

My mother brushes my hair back from my face. "Hush now, Katie."

My eyes are swollen and my nose is stuffed, making my voice sound nasaly and childlike. "W-w-what . . . am I . . . g-g-going to do, Mom?"

She smiles calmly, like she has all the answers. Like she has the power to take away any hurt—even this one—as easily as she used to kiss away the pain of my bumped shins and scraped knees. "You're going to sleep now. You're so tired."

She continues running her fingers through my hair. It's soothing. Relaxing. "Sleep now. . . . Go to sleep, my sweet, sweet girl."

My father taught me to play the guitar, but I get my voice from my mother. Lying in bed, I close my heavy eyes as she sings. It's a Melissa Etheridge song about angels knowing that everything will be all right. It's the same song she sang to me the night my father died—the night she slept in this bed with me. Because she couldn't bear to sleep in their bed alone.

With my mother's voice in my ears, I finally let go.

And fall asleep.

You know when you have a fever? And you lie in bed, and toss and roll and twist the sheets around your legs? You're not really sleeping, but you're not really awake either. There's moments of consciousness, when you open your eyes and realize with disoriented wonder that it's dark outside. But for the most part it's just a foggy blur.

That's what the next two days were like for me. A montage of sunlight and moonlight, of tears and vomiting and trays of food being taken away untouched.

The moments in that space between wakefulness and slumber were the hardest. When I'd start to believe it was all some horrible nightmare conjured from watching too many *90210* reruns. I'd feel a pillow against my back and swear it was Drew behind me. He gives the best wake-up calls—it's our own little tradition. Every morning he presses up against me and whispers in my ear, worshipping me with his words and with his hands.

But then I would open my eyes and see that the pillow was just a pillow. And it felt like a newly formed scab being torn off—I bled a little more each time.

There just aren't words to describe how I missed him. None that could even come close.

I physically ached for his smile, his scent, his voice.

Imagine a car's going sixty miles an hour down a country road and a tree falls and the car hits it. *Boom*—instant stoppage. But if the person in the driver's seat isn't wearing a seat belt? They're still going sixty.

And that's what love is like.

It doesn't just stop. No matter how hurt or wronged or angry you are—the love's still there.

Sending you right through the windshield.

On the evening of the second day, I open my eyes and stare out the window. It's drizzling.

Fitting—what with the black cloud over my head and everything.

Then I hear my bedroom door open. I roll over. "Mom, could you . . ."

Only it's not my mother standing there. My voice is quiet, softly surprised. "Oh—hey, George."

You remember George Reinhart, don't you? Steven's widower father? He and my mom are together. They hooked up at Matthew and Delores's wedding.

Don't worry—I've tried to block that part out too.

But they've been going strong about a year now. In spite of George's best efforts, my mother refuses to move to New York. She says Greenville is her home, that she likes her independence. So George comes down here pretty often to visit—weeks at a time. And my mom reciprocates when she can.

George is a good guy. He's kind of like Jimmy Stewart in *It's a Wonderful Life*—a little on the dorky side, sure, but decent. The kind of man you'd want looking after your mom.

His glasses sit crookedly on his face as he holds up a tray. "Your mother's swamped downstairs, but she thought you might like a cup of tea."

Running your own business isn't as easy as it looks. Yeah, you're your own boss—but that means no calling out sick, no playing hooky. And if an employee doesn't show up? You're the one who has to pick up the slack.

George tries hard to help out with the diner. Last week my mom had to drive our cook to the hospital after he sliced his hand open chopping potatoes. And George tried to fill in for him.

No one was injured—but the fire department had to come to put out flames, and the diner closed early because of the smoke.

Still, I guess it's the thought that counts.

I sit up and adjust the pillows behind me. "Tea would be great. Thank you."

He puts the tray on my nightstand and hands me a warm cup. Then he wipes his hands on his pants nervously.

"May I sit?"

I take a sip and nod. And George plops down in the beanbag chair beside my bed. He adjusts his glasses and wiggles around to get comfy.

I almost smile.

Then he looks at me for a few seconds, trying to find a way to start. I save him the trouble. "Mom told you, didn't she?"

He nods solemnly. "Don't be upset with her. She's worried about you, Kate. She needed to vent. I would never divulge your personal information to anyone." He taps his temple with one finger. "It's in the vault."

I actually manage to chuckle, because he reminds me so much of his son, Steven.

And then my smile fades, because he reminds me so much of Steven.

"John called me. Asking about you. I told him you were here."

My eyes rise sharply. Questioning.

"I didn't tell him why you were here—not exactly. I told him you were worn out. Burnt-out. It's not uncommon in our field."

I don't have a plan regarding the Evans. Technically, I'm carrying their grandchild, a part of their family. And even if their son feels otherwise, I have no doubt that Anne and John will want to be a part of its life.

But I can't think about that. Not yet.

George continues. "He'd like you to call him when you're feeling up to it. And he wanted me to tell you that he unequivocally rejects your resignation."

My brow furrows. "Can he do that?"

George shrugs. "John does what John wants."

Boy, does that sound familiar.

"He said he can't afford to lose both of his best investment bankers."

Wait—*both*?

"What does that mean? Has Drew not been going to work?"

A small, wishful flame flickers in my stomach. Maybe Drew is just as devastated as I am. Maybe he's gone into hibernation again—like he did the last time.

George quickly douses my poor little flame. "No, no, he's been there . . ."

Damn it.

". . . twice, actually. And drunker than a longshoreman on leave, from what I heard. When John asked him about your resignation letter, Drew told him to mind his own business—in his own colorful way, of course. Needless to say, his future at the firm is . . . fluid . . . at the moment."

I interpret this information the only way I can, considering who Drew was keeping company with the last time I saw him. "Wow. He must be having a really good time if he's still drunk the morning after."

George tilts his head to the side. "I wouldn't quite look at it that way, Kate."

I clench my jaw stubbornly. And lie. "It doesn't matter. I don't care anymore."

There's a moment of silence, and George stares at the pattern on the teacup. Then he purses his lips. And his voice is hushed—

reverent—like talking in church. "I don't know how much Drew told you about my Janey."

Quite a lot, actually. Janey Reinhart was a wonderful woman—kind, bright, warm.

She was diagnosed with breast cancer when Drew was ten and fought it for four years. Drew told me the day she passed away was the day he realized that bad things really happen—and not just to people you read about in the newspaper.

"When she died . . . I wanted to die too. And I would have, if it wasn't for Steven. Because that's what children are, Kate. Life renewed."

I know he means well. Really I do. But I can't handle this. I'm not ready to deal with the speech about how lucky I am to be pregnant.

And alone.

"Still . . . it was . . . awful. For a long time, it was just one terrible moment after the next. You know, Steven has his mother's eyes. Looking at him is like looking at Janey. And there were some days—really bad days—that I almost hated him for it."

I suck in a quick breath. This isn't the pep talk I was expecting.

"But still, time marched on. And things became . . . bearable. I gained a daughter-in-law and a beautiful granddaughter. And eventually, it didn't hurt to breathe."

Tears creep into my eyes. Because I know what he's saying. I know that pain.

"But it wasn't until I met your mother that the part of me that died with Janey came back to life. That I was whole again."

I rub my eyes dry and scoff, "So what are you telling me, George? I'll find another Drew again? It may just take fifteen years or so?"

Bitterness? Not attractive. Yeah—I know.

George's shakes his head slowly. "No, Kate. You'll never find another Drew. Just like I'll never have another Janey, and your mother will never have another Nate. But . . . what I'm trying to tell you is . . . the heart heals. And life goes on . . . and brings you with it . . . even if you don't want to go."

I bite my bottom lip. And nod my head. I put the cup back on the tray, ending the conversation. George pulls himself out of the beanbag chair and picks up the tray. He walks to the door, but he turns back to me before he goes through it.

"I know you probably don't want to hear this right now, but . . . I've known Drew his whole life. I watched him grow up with Matthew and Steven and Alexandra. I'm not defending him; I have no idea why he's made the choices he has. But . . . I can't help but feel sorry for him. Because one day he's going to open his eyes and realize that he's made the biggest mistake of his life. And because I love him like a son . . . the pain he's going to feel that day . . . well . . . it breaks my heart."

He's right.

I don't want to hear this. I don't have the patience to feel sorry for Drew.

But I appreciate his effort. "I'm really glad you're with my mom, George. I'm . . . grateful that she has you. Thank you."

He smiles warmly. "I'll be close by. Just give a call if you need anything."

I nod. And he closes the door behind him.

I want to be moved by George's words. Inspired. Motivated to drag my ass out of this bed. But I'm just too . . . tired. So I lay back down, wrap myself up in my blanket cocoon, and go to sleep.

On the third day, I rise again.

I don't really have much of a choice anymore. Lying around and breathing your own stench isn't exactly effective in lifting the spirits. Oh—and I've still been having morning sickness, like clockwork, in the same bucket my mother used to put beside my bed when I had a stomach virus. *Yummy.* Plus, I'm pretty sure if I squeeze my hair, I'll have enough grease to cook up a large fry at McDonald's.

Yeah—I'd say it's time to get up.

I drag myself to the bathroom, my movements stiff and slow. I take a long, hot shower—almost scalding. And the steam billows out behind me as I walk back into my room.

My mom's a saver. Not like the hoarders you see on that TLC show, but she's kept all the little mementos I didn't take with me to college and beyond.

See them? On those freshly dusted shelves? Little League trophies, science fair medals, and field day ribbons, next to framed photos of Delores, Billy, and me at graduation and Halloween and Delores's eighteenth birthday party.

I grab my bottle of body lotion out of my bag, but as the smell hits me I freeze. Vanilla and lavender. Drew's favorite scent. He can't get enough of it. Sometimes he drags his nose up my spine, sniffing and tickling me.

My chest tightens. And I toss the bottle in the trash can.

Glancing back to my bag, I notice my cell phone. It had been lying under the bottle of lotion, almost as if it were hiding on purpose.

It's been off since the flight. I consider calling Delores, but I quickly scrap that idea. Why ruin her vacation so she can rush home to commit premeditated murder?

Okay—you're right—I'm lying. I haven't called Delores because there's still a small, shriveled part of me that's hoping Drew will change his mind. That he'll find a way to fix this. And I won't have to give my best friend a reason to hate him. Well . . . another reason.

I turn the phone on to find four messages waving back at me. And there it is again.

Hope. It's becoming rather pathetic now, isn't it?

I bite my lip and take a steadying breath. And I punch in my code—praying to all the angels and saints that Drew's voice comes out of the speaker.

But of course it doesn't.

"Kate? It's Alexandra. I need you to call me right away."

I don't know why I'm surprised. Alexandra has a sixth sense when it comes to Drew. Don't get me wrong—she's first in line to hand him his ass when he screws up. But if she thinks he's in trouble? She swoops in like Batgirl on crack.

"Kate? Where are you and what the hell is going on with my brother? Call me back."

Drew and Alexandra are a lot alike. I wonder if it's genetic. Delayed gratification is not popular among the Evans offspring.

"Kate Brooks—don't you dare ignore my phone calls! I don't know what happened between you and Drew, but you just can't abandon someone like this! Jesus Christ, what's wrong with you? If these are your true colors, then . . . then he's better off without you!"

Neither, apparently, is emotional stability. I could say her words don't bother me—but I'd be lying. That last line hurt.

One more message to go.

"Kate . . . it's Alexandra again . . ."

Her voice is different. Less urgent and impatient.

Almost a whisper.

". . . I'm sorry. I shouldn't have yelled like that. I'm just worried. He won't talk to me, Kate. He's never not talked to me before. I don't

*know what's going on between you two . . . and I don't need to know,
but . . . just . . . please come back? Whatever happened . . . wherever
you are . . . I know you two can work it out. You don't have to call
me . . . just . . . please . . . please come home. He loves you, Kate . . .
so much."*

I stare at the phone, breathing hard. Of course Drew won't
talk to her. There's no way in hell he's going to look his pregnant
sister in the eye and tell her he all but kicked me out because I'm
pregnant too.

He's a lot of things. Stupid isn't one of them.

I throw the phone across the room out of self-preservation,
because I *want* to call. I *want* to go back. But apparently I do have
some dignity left, even if it's just a shred. Why should I extend
the olive branch? I'm not the one who burnt down the tree. John
knows where I am now. If Drew wants me, it won't be hard for him
to find me.

I push my hands through my quickly drying hair and open my
closet door. And there, staring back at me, is my good, old waitress
uniform—plaid skirt, lace top, white cowgirl hat.

It's been ten years since I last wore it. I take out the hanger,
smiling. I had a lot of good times in this uniform.

Easy, uncomplicated times.

I put it on—like a bride trying on her wedding dress a year
after the wedding—just to see if it still fits. It does. And as I look
at myself in the full-length mirror, I know just what I'm going to
do next. Because routine is good. Any routine. Even an old one.

I may not have a plan for the rest of my life.

But at least I've got one for the rest of today.

Feeling a lot less like a corpse than I have the last few days, I make my way toward the back stairs that lead to the break room. On the second step, I overhear my mom and George talking below.

Brace yourselves, this one's a doozy.

"Goddamn him! Who does he think he is? When Billy and Kate broke up, I was relieved—a blind man could've seen that they had grown apart. And when . . . when she introduced me to Drew, I thought he was perfect for her. That he was more . . . like her. A part of the world she lives in now. And the way he looked at her, George. It was so obvious he adored her. How can he *treat* her like this!?"

George's voice is calm. Understanding. "I know. I . . ."

My mother cuts him off, and I imagine she's pacing. "No! No. He's not going to get away with this. I'm going to . . . I'm going to call his mother!"

George sighs. "I hardly think that's what Kate would want you to do, Carol. They're adults—"

My mother's voice rises, high-pitched and protective. "She's not an adult to me! She's my baby! And she's hurting. He broke her heart . . . and . . . I don't know if she's going to get through this. It's like she's just . . . given up."

I hear a hand slap against the wood table. "That little . . . punk! He's a foul-mouthed, smart-ass little punk. And he's not going to get away with this!" Her tone is determined.

And a little scary.

"You're right—I won't call Anne. I'm going to New York myself. I'll show him what happens when you mess with my daughter. He'll think Amelia Warren is Mother Fucking Teresa when I'm done with him. I'll rip his balls off!"

Holy Moley.

Okay, my mother? Doesn't curse. Ever. So the fact that she's dropping f-bombs and talking about the ripping off of balls?

Frankly, it's disturbing.

I walk down the rest of the steps, like I haven't heard a thing. "Morning."

My mother's face is slack. Shocked. "Kate. You're up."

I nod. "Yes. I'm feeling . . . better."

Better might be too strong. Resurrected road kill is more accurate.

George offers me a mug. "Coffee?"

My hand covers my queasy stomach. "No, thanks."

My mother shakes off her surprise and asks, "How about some warm Coca-Cola?"

"Yeah. That sounds good."

She gets it for me. Then she smooths my hair down as she says, "When I was pregnant with you, I was sick for seven months. Warm Coca-Cola always made me feel better. Plus if it comes back up, it doesn't taste all that bad."

She's got a point.

FYI—peanut butter? So not fun the second time around.

My mother's brow wrinkles as she notices the uniform. "Are all your clothes dirty? Do you need me to do some laundry?"

"No, I just thought I'd help out in the diner today. You know—keep busy. So I don't have too much time to think."

Thinking is bad. Thinking is very, very bad.

George smiles.

My mom rubs my arm. "As long as you're feeling up to it. Mildred is working today, so I could certainly use the help."

Mildred has worked at our restaurant for as long as I can remember. She's a terrible waitress—I think my mother just keeps her on out of charity. Legend says that she was once a beauty queen—Miss Kentucky, or Louisiana, or something like that. But she lost her looks and her zest for life when her fiancé played chicken with an oncoming freight train. And lost.

Now she lives in the apartment complex downtown, and smokes two packs a day.

But she'll probably live to be a hundred and seven—compared to the thirty-one-year-old mother of three who's never touched a cigarette a day in her life, yet somehow still dies from lung cancer.

Like I said, God? He's a real sick son of a bitch sometimes.

Waitressing skills are like riding a bike—you never really forget.

Though there are a few close calls, I manage to get through the morning without vomiting in any of the customers' pancake platters or scrambled eggs.

Golf clap for me.

The toughest part is the questions. About New York—about my handsome boyfriend who came here with me to visit three months ago. I smile and keep my answers short and vague.

By noon, I'm pretty much wiped out. Physically and mentally. I'm just about to retreat to my room for a nap when the bell above the door rings, and a voice comes from behind me.

A voice I would know anywhere.

Chapter 10

"Katie Brooks in a cowgirl uniform. Is this for real, or some freakishly vivid acid flashback?"

I was six years old the first time I laid eyes on Billy Warren. Around the same time that Joey Martino was abandoning Amelia in that hotel room? Her younger sister, Sophie, was being kicked out of the house.

Because she was pregnant too.

Apparently the elder Mrs. Warren subscribed to the *Mommie Dearest* style of parenting—wire hangers and all. Anyway, five years later, Sophie died in a drug den from a meth overdose. The state took custody of Billy until they were able to track down his only living relative, Amelia Warren.

Delores stayed with us for the weekend while her mother went to California to get him. Amelia walked into the group home and saw a small, hollow-eyed little boy in a ripped black T-shirt. And from that moment on, Billy was hers—even though she hadn't given birth to him.

For the first four months that Billy lived with Amelia and Delores, he didn't speak. At all. He followed us around, did everything we did. When we played school he was the chalkboard, when we dug for buried treasure, he was our pack mule.

But he didn't talk.

And then one day Amelia was running errands on Main Street, and they passed a pawn shop. Billy stopped in his tracks. And stared into the front window.

At a shiny red guitar.

Amelia went in and bought it for him. By this time I was pretty good at playing, so she figured my father could give Billy lessons too. But—here's the thing—before my dad got around to giving him even one lesson? Billy already knew how to play. He was a prodigy, like Mozart. A true musical genius.

He can be really annoying about it sometimes.

"Billy!"

I throw my arms around his neck. He squeezes me tight at the waist and my feet leave the floor. My voice is muffled by his shoulder. "God, it's good to see you!"

I know you think he's a dick. But he's not. Really.

You've only seen him through Drew-colored glasses.

Billy pulls back, his hands on my upper arms. It's been about eight months since I saw him last. He's toned and tan—healthy. He looks good. Except for the beard. I'm not digging the beard. It's thick and shaggy—reminds me of a lumberjack.

"You too, Katie. You look . . ." His brow furrows. And his smile turns into a frown. "God*damn*. You look like day-old shit."

Yep, that's Billy. He always did know just what to say to a girl.

"Wow. With lines like that, you must be beating them off with a bat in LA. By the way—you know there's a rat hanging off your face?"

He laughs and rubs his beard. "It's my disguise. I need one now, you know."

On cue, a boy who looks to be about ten approaches us hesitantly. "Can I have your autograph, Mr. Warren?"

Billy's grin widens. And he takes the offered pen and paper. "Sure thing." He scribbles quickly, hands the autograph back, and says, "Don't stop dreaming, kid—they really do come true."

After the starstruck boy walks away, Billy turns back to me, eyes sparkling. "How fucking cool is that?"

He's the hottest thing in music these days. His last album stayed at number one for six weeks—and there's big Grammy buzz for this year's awards. I'm proud of him. He's right where I always believed he could be.

Still, I tease, "Careful. You still have to get that big head back out the door."

He chuckles. "What are you doing here? I was supposed to come to the city to see you guys next week."

Before I can answer, a face appears out of thin air on the other side of the glass door.

Scaring the ever-loving shit out of me. "Ah!"

It's a light-haired woman with huge, unblinking brown eyes. Kind of like ET in the blond wig.

Billy turns. "Oh—that's Evay."

"Evie?"

"No, E-vay. Like eBay. She's with me." He opens the door and ET girl walks in, hands folded tightly at her waist. She's wearing black leggings and a Bob Marley T-shirt. The word skinny doesn't even come close. She reminds me of one of those skeletons in biology class, with a thin, flesh-colored coating.

She's kind of pretty—in a concentration camp kind of way.

"Evay, this is Kate. Kate—Evay."

In the professional world, handshakes are important. They give prospective clients a sneak peek at how you do business. They can make or break a deal. I always make sure my grip is firm—strong. Just because I'm petite and a woman doesn't mean I'm gonna get stepped on.

"It's nice to meet you, Evay." I hold out my hand.

She just stares at it—like it's a spider crawling out of the shower drain. "I don't make direct female-to-female contact. It depletes the beautification cells."

O-kay. I glance at Billy. He seems unperturbed. I hook a thumb over my shoulder. "So . . . do you guys want to eat? How about a booth?"

When Evay answers, her tone is airy, dazed, like a concussion victim. Or an acting coach—*be the tree.*

"I have my lunch right here." She opens her palm to reveal an assortment of capsules that make my prenatals look like baby candy. "But I need water. Do you have clear water from a snowy mountain spring?"

Wow.

Somebody call Will Smith—aliens really have landed.

"Uh . . . we don't get much snow around here, this time of year. We have Greenville's finest tap water, though."

She shakes her head. And she still hasn't blinked. Not *one freaking* time.

"I only drink snowy mountain spring water."

Billy raises his hand. "I'm jonesin' for some onion rings."

I smile and put in his order. "Sure."

Evay sniffs the air, like a squirrel before a storm. Then she looks a little petrified. "Is that grease? Do you cook with actual grease?"

I take a step back. She might be one of those wacked-out, PETA-loving vegan people who are offended by animal byproducts—and the prospect of being doused with red paint isn't too appealing at the moment.

"Ah . . . yes?"

She covers her nose with bony fingers. "I can't breathe this air! I'll break out!" She turns to the door.

And waits.

Guess females aren't the only thing she doesn't make contact with.

Billy opens it for her and she scurries out. I look at him, flabbergasted. "Okay, what the hell was *that*?"

"*That* was a Californian. They're all like that. I think it's from too much sun . . . and weed. They make Dee Dee look fucking mundane. Plus Evay's a model, so she's an extra-large kind of weird. She won't smell grease, but she smokes like a chimney."

That's why I'm happy I live in New York.

Where the normal people are.

Well . . . lived, anyway.

I walk behind the counter to get a take-out box for Billy's rings. He rests his elbows on the counter, leaning over. "So where's Dr. Manhattan?"

He means Drew. You know—after the arrogant, inhuman, blue physicist in the *Watchmen* comics?

"He's not here."

Billy looks surprised. Pleasantly so. "No kidding? I didn't think he let you out of his sight, let alone out of the state. What's up with that?"

I shrug. "Long story."

"Sounds promising. Hey—let's hang out later. Catch up. I have to get Evay back to the hotel for her nap, then I'll swing back and pick you up."

My eyes squint. "Her nap?"

He lifts his chin defensively. "Yeah. Lots of people sleep twelve hours during the day."

I hand him his onion rings. "I know. They're called vampires, Billy."

He laughs.

And then my mother walks out of the kitchen. "Billy! Amelia said you were visiting."

She hugs him and he kisses her cheek. "Hey, Carol."

She looks disapprovingly at his beard. "Oh honey, you have such a handsome face. Don't cover it up with all . . . this."

My mother is such a mom, isn't she?

Billy defends his facial hair. "Why's everyone hating on the beard? I like the beard." Then he holds out a hundred-dollar bill. "For the onion rings."

She shakes her head and pushes his hand back. "Your money's no good here—you know that."

A crash of breaking glass comes from behind the kitchen door. And George Reinhart's voice: "Carol!"

My mother clicks her tongue. "Oh, dear. George is trying to work the dishwasher again."

She runs off to the kitchen. Billy and I share a laugh. Then he hands me the hundred-dollar bill. "Slip this into the register when your mom's not looking, okay?"

It's tough when you get to the point in your life—like we have—when you're able to help the parentals financially, but they're too stubborn to accept.

"Sure thing."

He taps the counter. "Okay, four o'clock, I'll pick you up. Be ready. And don't wear any power suit or shit like that—this is a strictly jeans and sneaks kind of mission."

That's what I'd planned on. But still I have to ask, "Why? What are we gonna to do?"

He shakes his head at me. "You've been gone too long, Katie-girl. What else would we do? We're goin' womping."

Right. Silly me. Of course we are.

Billy leans over the counter and kisses my cheek quickly. "Later."

Then he grabs his take-out and walks out the door.

Have you ever gone for a ride in your car, after your last final exam or the beginning of a long weekend from work? And the road's wide open, your sunglasses are on, and your favorite song is blaring out of the speakers?

Good. Then you know just what this feels like.

Womping.

How to explain it? I'm sure there're various names for it, depending on where you live, but here, that's what we call it. It's like mountain climbing . . . only . . . with a car. Or a truck. Or any other automobile with four-wheel drive.

The goal is to scale a hill, the steepest you can find, and get as vertical as you can, as fast as you can, *without* flipping the car. It's fun—in a stupid, dangerous, adrenaline-junkie kind of way.

Don't worry about my delicate condition. Billy's truck is an off-road vehicle with safety harnesses instead of seatbelts. So even if we flip? I'm not going anywhere.

We're riding out to the hills right now, full speed ahead. Ohio isn't exactly known for its hilly terrain, but there are a few spots where these abound. Lucky for us, Greenville is near them.

The windows are open, the sun is bright, and it's a comfortable seventy degrees. I yell above the sound of the stereo, "So . . . another new car?"

Billy smiles and rubs his hand lovingly across the dash. "Yep. And this baby's unpolluted by my cousin's evil handiwork."

I roll my eyes. I definitely need to check out Billy's financial portfolio. The wind whips my hair around my face. I push it back and yell again, "Don't be that guy."

"What guy?"

"The guy that has a different car for every day of the month. Spend your money on more practical things."

He shrugs. "I told Amelia I'd buy her a house. As long as she doesn't tell Delores where it is."

Billy and Delores love to rag on each other.

The song on the radio changes, and Billy turns it up to maximum volume. He looks at me. And he's smiling.

We both are.

Because, once upon a time, it was our song. Not in a romantic way. In a teenager, rebel-without-a-cause kind of way. It was our anthem; our "Thunder Road."

Alabama sings about getting out of a small town, beating the odds, living for love. We belt out the lyrics together.

It's great. It's perfect.

Billy pushes the gas pedal to the floor, leaving a cloud of dust behind us, and I remember how it feels to be sixteen again. When life was easy, and the most pressing matter was where we could hang out on a Friday night.

They say youth is wasted on the young—and they're right.

But it's not the youths' fault. No matter how often they're told to appreciate the days they're living, they just can't.

Because they have nothing to compare it to. It's only later, when it's too late—when there're bills to pay and deadlines to make—that they realize how sweet, how innocent and precious, those moments were.

The singer croons about Thunderbirds, and driving all night, and living your own life. Billy's first car was a Thunderbird. You got a glimpse of it in New York, remember? It was a junker when he bought it, but he fixed it up himself on weekends and during the many days he blew off school.

I lost my virginity in its backseat. Prom weekend. Yes—I'm a statistic. At the time, I thought it was the epitome of romance, the peak of perfection.

But—again—I didn't have anything else to compare it to.

Billy loved that car. And I'd bet my business degree he's still got it in his garage in LA.

Still singing, I hold on to the harness straps with both hands as Billy spins the car into a 360-degree turn. It's a terrific maneuver. You floor the gas pedal, jerk the steering wheel, and pull up on the emergency break. It's the best way to do a donut—as long as the transmission doesn't drop out the bottom of your car or anything.

Dust billows up from the ground, and dirt scatters across the windshield. It's always been this way with us. Comfortable. Uncomplicated. Well—at least when we were here in Greenville, it was.

As I went through college and business school, we drifted. Became less Bonnie and Clyde and more Wendy and Peter Pan. But out here, when it was just the two of us and the rest of the world didn't exist, we could be those kids again. Kids who wanted the same things, who dreamed the same dreams.

The wheels spin and Billy peels out across a flat, unpaved piece of land. And it feels like we're flying. Like I'm free. Not a care in the world.

And the best part? For the first time in almost four days, I don't think about Drew Evans at all.

Chapter 11

By the time we make it back to Billy's motel room, it's dark. We stumble through the door—tired and dusty and laughing. I plop down on the couch while Billy picks up a piece of paper from the kitchenette counter.

"Where's Evay?"

He holds up the note. "She took a car back to LA. She said the unprocessed air was invading her pores."

"You don't look too broken up about it."

He gets two beers from the fridge and shrugs. "There's more where she came from. No shit off my shoe."

Billy picks up the guitar lying across the coffee table and strums a few chords. Then he reaches under the cushion and takes out a clear plastic baggie. He tosses it to me. "You still roll the best joints this side of the Mississippi—or has the establishment completely assimilated you into the collective?"

I smirk and pick up the bag. Rolling a good joint takes concentration. Use too much weed and it's just wasteful—too little and you defeat the purpose.

It's a relaxing process. Like knitting.

I lick the edge of the paper and smooth it down. Then I pass it to Billy.

He looks at it admiringly. "You're an artist."

He puts the joint between his lips and flips open his Zippo. But before the flame touches the tip, I snap the metal cap closed.

"Don't. I could get a contact high."

"So?"

I sigh. And look Billy straight in the face. "I'm pregnant."

His eyes go wide. And the joint falls from his lips.

"No shit?"

I shake my head. "No shit, Billy."

His turns forward, staring at the table. He doesn't say anything for several moments, so I fill the dead air.

"Drew doesn't want it. He told me to have an abortion."

The words come out detached. Flat. Because I still can't believe they're true.

Billy turns back to me and hisses, "What?"

I nod. And fill him in on the more sordid details of my departure from New York. By the time I'm finished, he's on his feet, pissed off and pacing. He mumbles, "That motherfucker owes me a gun."

"What?"

He waves me off. "Nothing." Then he sits down and pushes a hand through his hair. "I knew he was an asshole—I fucking *knew* it. I really didn't take him for a Garrett Buckler, though."

Every town has two sides of the tracks—the good side and the not-so-good side. Garrett Buckler came from the good side of Greenville, with its automatic sprinklers and stucco-sided McMansions. He was a senior, our sophomore year in high school. And from the first day of school that year, Garrett was focused on one thing: Dee Dee Warren.

Billy hated him on sight. He's always been distrustful of people with money—money they didn't earn themselves. And Garrett was no exception. But Delores blew Billy off. Told him he was being ridiculous. Paranoid. Said she wanted to give Garrett a chance.

So she did. She also gave him her virginity.

And four weeks later, behind the bleachers at school, Delores told Garrett she was pregnant. Apparently we Greenville women are quite the Fertile Myrtles.

Don't spit on us—you might knock us up.

And yes, despite all the sex education Amelia gave us, it still happened. Because—here's the thing a lot of people forget about teenagers—sometimes they just do stupid things. Not because they don't have the education or resources, but because they're too damn young to really understand that actions have consequences.

Life-changing ones.

Anyway, as you can imagine, Delores was terrified. But like any moon-eyed, romantic, adolescent girl, she figured Garrett would be there for her. That they'd get through whatever was coming together.

She was wrong. He told her to fuck off. He accused her of trying to trap him—said he didn't believe that the kid was even his.

History's a lot like shampoo that way—rinse, repeat, and repeat again.

Delores was crushed. And Billy . . . Billy was fucking furious. I was with him the day he stole a white Camaro from the Walgreen's parking lot. I followed him in the Thunderbird to a chop shop in Cleveland, where he got paid three hundred dollars for it.

Just enough to pay for the abortion.

We could've gone to Amelia, but Delores was just too ashamed. So we went to the clinic ourselves. And I held Delores's hand the whole time.

Afterward, Billy dropped us off at my house. Then he went looking for Garrett Buckler. When he found him, Billy broke his arm and fractured his jaw. And he told him if he ever breathed a word about Delores to anyone, he'd come back and break his other four appendages—including the one between his legs.

To this day, it's the best-kept secret in Greenville.

"You know what? Fuck him. You make good cash, so you sure as shit don't need his money. And as for the whole dad thing? Overrated. You had a father for like, five minutes . . . me and my cousin never did. And the three of us turned out great."

He rethinks that statement.

"Okay—maybe not Delores. But still—two out of three ain't bad. We could—"

I cut him off. "I think I'm gonna get an abortion, Billy."

He goes silent. Totally. Utterly.

Completely.

But his shock and disappointment pound loudly—like a big bass drum.

Or maybe that's just my own guilt.

Remember about twenty years ago, when that Susan Smith lady drowned her two children, because her boyfriend didn't want a woman with kids? Like the rest of the country, I thought she should've been strung up by her fingertips and had the skin scraped off her body with a cheese grater.

I mean, what kind of woman does that? What kind of woman chooses a man over her own flesh and blood?

A weak one.

And that's a characteristic I've already admitted to, remember?

It's been in my mind for a while now—like a cobweb that's clinging to a corner but you walk on past because you just don't have the time to deal with it.

I'm a businesswoman, first and foremost. I'm analytical. Practical.

If one of my investments isn't turning out the way I thought it would? I get rid of it. Cut my losses. Simple mathematics—if you take the emotion out of it, it's a no brainer.

I know. I know what you're thinking. *But what about that little boy you pictured? That beautiful, perfect boy with dark hair and the smile you love?*

The truth is, there is no little boy. Not yet. Right now, it's nothing more than a cluster of dividing cells. A mistake that's standing in the way of me and the life I was supposed to have.

I don't know if Drew and I can ever get back to where we were—but I know giving birth to a child he obviously wants nothing to do with isn't going to win me any points. And it would make everything so much easier.

Like getting my eyebrows waxed. A simple procedure for a lifetime of convenience.

You think that makes me a cold bitch, don't you?

Yeah . . . well . . . I guess you're right.

Billy's voice is cautious. Hesitant. Like he doesn't want to ask the question, and he wants to hear the answer even less. "For him? You're gonna get an abortion because of him?"

I wipe at the wetness on my cheeks. I didn't even know I was crying. "I can't do this on my own. Alone."

It always comes back to that, doesn't it?

Billy grabs my hand. "Hey. Look at me."

I do.

And his eyes are burning. With tenderness. And determination. "You are not alone, Kate. And you never will be. Not as long as I'm breathing."

I bite my lip. And shake my head slowly. And the lump in my throat makes my voice raspy and frail. "You know what I mean, Billy."

And he does. Billy understands better than anyone, because he was there. He knows how hard it was, how bad it felt. All those nights when I went out with him, for ice cream or to the movies—leaving my mother home in an empty house.

All the awards and graduation ceremonies, when my mother's face glowed with pride, but her eyes shone with sadness. Because she had no one to share it with.

Every holiday—New Year's Eves and Thanksgivings and Easters—when I couldn't make it home from college, and I'd cry in his arms after getting off the phone with her, because it killed me that she was spending the day by herself.

Billy was there for all of it.

And Amelia. He saw his aunt struggle—financially, emotionally—trying to be two parents in one for him and Delores. He watched her date guy after guy, looking for a Mr. Right who never showed up.

Theirs were the anti-lives. The ones I never wanted for my own.

And yet, here I am.

Billy nods. "Yeah, Katie—I know what you mean."

I rub my eyes hard. Frustrated. Aggravated . . . with myself. "I just need to make a goddamn decision. I have to figure out a plan and stick with it. I just . . ." My voice breaks. "I just don't know what to do."

Billy breathes deep. Then he stands up. "All right, screw this. Let's go."

He walks around the corner and digs into the cabinet under the kitchen sink. I have no idea what he's looking for.

"What do you mean? Go where?"

He pops up holding up a screwdriver. "To the place where our problems can't touch us."

Billy pulls the truck into the parking lot. And the headlights illuminate the huge, darkened sign.

Can you see it?

ROLLER RINK

We climb out. "I don't think this is a good idea, Billy."

"Why not?"

We walk to the side of the building. Here's some advice I learned young: When you're walking in the dark? Or running from the cops through the woods? Step high. It'll save your shins and the palms of your hands a world of pain.

"Because we're adults now. This is breaking and entering."

"It was breaking and entering when we were seventeen too."

We get to the window. I can just barely make out Billy's face in the moonlight.

"I know. But I don't think Sheriff Mitchell's going to be so quick to let us off the hook now."

He scoffs. "Oh, please. Amelia said Mitchell's been bored out of his gourd since we left. He'd kill for some excitement. Kids today . . . too lazy. There's no creativity to their vandalism."

Wait. What?

Let's back up a moment.

"What do you mean, 'Amelia said'? Since when does Amelia talk to Sheriff Mitchell?"

Billy shakes his head. "Trust me—you don't want to know." He holds up the screwdriver. "You still got it? Or have you lost your touch?"

For the second time tonight, I accept his challenge. I snatch the screwdriver and walk up to the window. And under twenty seconds later, we're inside.

Oh, yeah—I've still got it.

The roller rink was our place: breaking in after closing, our national pastime. Idle hands really are the devil's tools. So—for God's sake—get your kids a hobby.

Ten minutes later I'm flying across the slick floor in worn, size-six skates.

It's a wonderful feeling. Like floating on air—spinning on big, puffy clouds.

The stereo system plays the eighties' greatest hits in the background. Billy leans against the wall—toking up and blowing the smoke out the open window.

He inhales deeply. And tufts of white puff out from his lips as he says, "You know, you could come to California with me. Set up your own shop. I have friends—guys with money—they'd invest with you. My friends are your friends. *Mi casa es su casa*—and all that."

I stop sliding as I consider his words. "Actually, that means, 'My house is your house.'"

Billy's eyebrows come together. "Oh." He shrugs. "I always did suck in Spanish. Señorita Gonzales hated me."

"That's because you crazy-glued her Lhasa Apsos together."

He giggles, remembering. "Oh, yeah. That was a great night."

I chuckle too. And go into a spin that any Olympic ice skater would be proud of. The song changes to "Never Say Goodbye" by Bon Jovi. It was our prom song.

Raise your hand if it was yours too. I'm pretty sure, after 1987, it's been the prom song of every high school in America at least once.

Billy snuffs out the joint with his fingertips. Then skates up to me. He holds out his arm, doing his best Beetlejuice impression.

"Shall we?"

I smile. And take his arm. I put my hands on his shoulders, and while Bon Jovi sings about smoky rooms and losing keys, we start to sway.

Billy's hands sit low on my back. I turn my head and rest my cheek against his chest. He's warm. His flannel shirt is soft and smells like pot and earth . . . and home. I feel his chin against the top of my head as he asks me quietly, "Remember prom?"

I smile. "Yeah. Remember Dee Dee's dress?"

He laughs. Because Delores was the original trendsetter—even then. Lady Gaga's got nothing on her. Her dress was white and stiff, like a ballerina's tutu. And it had a string of twinkling lights along the hem. It was really pretty.

Until it caught on fire.

Her date, Louis Darden, put it out with the punch bowl of spiked Kool-Aid. She spent the rest of the night sticky and smelling like a doused campfire.

I continue our trek down memory lane. "Remember the last day of junior year?"

Billy's chest rumbles as he snickers. "Not my stealthiest moment."

It was the final day of school—and about one hundred and three degrees inside our sadly under-air-conditioned school. But

Principal Cleeves refused to let us out early. So Billy pulled the fire alarm.

Right down the hall from where the principal was standing.

A hot pursuit ensued, but Billy successfully avoided capture. So the principal went on the intercom system and tried paging him. *"Billy Warren, please report to the main office. Immediately."*

"I know I'm not the brightest bulb in the box, but come on. Did they really think I was stupid enough to actually go?"

I laugh against Billy's shirt. "And then as soon as you walked in senior year, Cleeves grabbed you and was all like, 'Mr. Warren, there's a chair in detention with your name on it.'"

And there really was. They stenciled his name on the back of a chair, like a director's chair on a movie set.

Billy sighs. "Good times."

I nod. "The best."

And as words about favorite songs and loves that would never end swirl around us, I close my eyes. Billy's arms tighten around me just a bit, pulling me closer.

Do you see where this is going? I didn't.

"I've missed this, Katie. I miss you."

I don't say it back, but it's nice to hear. And it's even nicer to be held.

To be wanted.

I haven't felt anything more than friendly affection for Billy in a long, long time. But that doesn't mean I've forgotten. The girl I used to be. The one who thought there was nothing sweeter than looking into Billy Warren's eyes. Nothing more romantic than hearing him sing. Nothing more exciting than riding in his car, late at night, after curfew.

I remember what it feels like to love him. Even though I don't love him in quite the same way anymore.

I gaze up at Billy's face as he sings the song's words softly. To me.

Looking back now, I'm not exactly sure who leaned where, who moved first. All I know is one minute we were dancing in the middle of the skating rink . . . and the next, Billy was kissing me.

And it only took a second before I was kissing him back.

Chapter 12

Kissing Billy is . . . nice. It's familiar. Sweet.

Like finding your old Strawberry Shortcake house in your parents' attic. And you smile when you see it. You run your hand over the balcony and remember all the days you spent wrapped up in its make-believe world. It's nostalgic. A part of your childhood.

But it's a part you've left behind. Because you're a grown-up now.

So no matter how dear the memories are, you're not going to bust out Apple Dumplin' and Plum Puddin' and start playing.

The kiss ends and I lower my head. And I stare at Billy's shirt. You know that line—I think it's from a song—if you can't be with the one you love, love the one you're with?

That could fit really well in this situation.

Except for the fact that I already love Billy. Too much to take advantage of his devotion—too much to use him to heal my broken heart and bruised ego. He deserves better than that. Billy Warren is no one's consolation prize. And I'd happily scratch the eyes out of any woman who tried to make him one.

He once told me I wasn't the girl he fell in love with anymore. And as much as it hurt to hear, as inadequate as it made me feel at the time—he was right.

I'm not that girl anymore.

I drag my eyes from his shirt to his face. "Billy . . ."

He puts his finger to my lips, brushing them softly. He closes his eyes and takes a breath. Neither of us moves for a moment, caught up for a few final seconds in the enchantment of the past.

Then he speaks, breaking the spell. "Being here with you? It's awesome. As good as I remember—better, even. It feels . . . it feels like we got to take a ride in the DeLorean." His hand holds my face tenderly. "But it's okay, Kate. It was just for a minute. And now we're back to the future. It doesn't have to mean anything more than that. It doesn't have to change what we have now, 'cause that's pretty awesome too."

I nod, relieved. Thankful that Billy knows what I feel without me having to say the words. And that he feels the same.

"Okay."

He smiles. "I should get you home, before Carol calls out the dogs. Or worse—Amelia."

I chuckle. And hand in hand, we leave the roller-skating rink and all of its memories behind.

Twenty minutes later, Billy pulls into the back parking lot of my mother's diner. We sit in the truck silently, side by side.

"You want me to walk you up?"

"No—it's all right. I can manage."

He nods slowly. "So . . . is there gonna be like . . . weirdness between us now? Because we tongue-wrestled for a couple minutes?"

Like I said before—Billy always did have a way with words.

"No. No weirdness. No worries."

He needs further confirmation. "You still my girl, Katie?"

He doesn't mean in the girlfriend way. He means in the friend—the *best* friend, who *happens* to be a girl—kind of way. In case you were wondering.

"I'll always be your girl, Billy."

"Good." He turns his head to the windshield and looks out. "You should really think about California. I think it would be a nice change for you. A clean break."

He's right, in a way. California would be a blank page for me. No memories. No painful run-ins. No awkward conversations. And with my résumé, I don't foresee finding a new job to be too much of a problem.

That being said . . . I have connections in New York. Roots. And I'm not sure I want to sever all of them. So like every other aspect of my life at the moment, I don't know what the hell I want to do.

Sound like a broken record, don't I? Sorry.

I put my hand over his on the gearshift. "I'll think about it."

He puts his other hand on top of mine. "You'll figure it out, Kate—I know you will. And it gets better. You won't hurt like this forever. I speak from experience."

I smile gratefully. "Thanks, Billy. For everything." Then I climb out of the truck and he drives away.

After letting my mother know I'm back, I head to my room. I shut the door behind me and lean against it. Exhausted.

Talk about a long frigging day.

My mother's cleaned my room. Not that it was messy before, but I can tell. The pillows are fluffed just a bit more, and my cell phone sits neatly on the nightstand.

I kick off my shoes, pick it up, and turn it on. Despite my hissy fit earlier, it still works. I stare at the numbers. They're lit up. Calling to me. Taunting me.

It would be so easy. Just ten quick digits and I could hear his voice. It's been forever since I heard his voice. My hands shake a little. Like a junkie, needing a fix—just a taste.

Do you think he'd pick up?

Do you think he'd be alone if he did?

And that's the thought that kills the craving. There's no way I'm calling.

Still . . . I don't listen to my voicemails often. Usually I just check the missed call list. I delete my voicemails even less.

I scroll down the screen, to the date I need.

And press play.

"Hey, babe. The golf outing ran over. I was gonna stop and pick up a bottle for later. You want Dom or Philipponnat? You know what? On second thought—screw the Champagne. You taste better than both of them put together. I'll be home in five minutes."

I close my eyes and let his words wash over me. Drew has an amazing voice. Calm and soothing—but devilishly seductive at the same time. He totally could've gone into radio.

I press another button.

This time his tone is teasing. *"Kaate, you're late. Tell Delores to pick out her own goddamn shoes. You've got a boyfriend who's sitting in a big, frothy Jacuzzi all by his lonesome. Come home, sweetheart. I'm here waiting for you."*

If only that was true today.

There's more—some are quick and to the point, some are downright dirty. And I listen to every single one. He doesn't say "I love you" in any of them—but he doesn't have to. I hear it in every word. Every time he says my name.

And I can't help but wonder how this all happened? How did we get here? And can we ever go back?

I don't cry. There just aren't any tears left. I curl up in the middle of my bed. And Drew's voice lulls me to sleep.

The next afternoon, Billy and I are in the back room of the diner, sharing a plate of fries. He's working on a new song and he thinks better on his feet.

See him there? Walking from one end of the room to the other, mumbling and humming, and occasionally strumming the guitar strapped across his chest?

I sit at the table. Trying to think my way out of the pit of despair that is now my life.

As Billy crosses toward the door that leads to the diner, something catches his eye in the round window at the top. And he backs away. "Oh, shit."

I look up. "What? What's wrong?"

Then the door bursts open. It slams against the wall and then stays in place—afraid to move an inch. Because there, standing in the doorway in all her pissed-off glory, is my best friend.

Delores Warren.

Oh, shit indeedy.

She's wearing red knee-high leather boots, tight black pants, an embellished black top, and a short, black-and-white faux fur jacket. A myriad of Louis Vuitton bags hang off her shoulders, matching the large wheeled one trailing behind her.

And the anger in her amber eyes makes them sparkle like fresh-cut topaz stones . "Does someone want to tell me why I had to hear from *my mother* that there was a Three Musketeers' reunion going on in Greenville that I wasn't invited to?"

She stomps forward. Billy moves behind my chair, using me like a human shield.

"Or better yet—would anyone like to explain why my best friend took off from New York like a bat out of hell, leaving behind a shit storm that makes Sandy look like an April-fucking-shower—and I have no idea why?!"

She takes another step forward and drops her bags to the floor. Then she snaps her head to the right—in the direction of the perky blond teenager standing next to the lockers.

That's Kimberly. She's a waitress here. Works after school. She's seems nice.

And at the moment—terrified.

"Hey, Gidget, how about you make yourself useful and get me a Diet Coke? Don't scrimp on the ice."

Kimberly flees the room.

Lucky girl.

Delores points at me and yells, like Jack Nicholson in *A Few Good Men*, "Well?! You can't keep me out of the loop, Kate. *I am the loop!*"

My voice comes out meek. Repentant. If you're ever in the attack range of an angry she-wolf, lay down and play dead. It'll go easier that way.

"I didn't want to ruin your vacation."

Delores snorts, "If only Queen Bee-atch Alexandra had been so thoughtful. She called us twenty times at the hotel—freaking out about how we had to come home because Drew needed a suicide watch."

I roll my eyes. "She's exaggerating."

"I thought so too. Until I saw the Dark Prince myself. Wasn't pretty."

I take the news like a newborn bird to a worm, greedy for more. "You saw Drew? What did he say? Did he ask about me?"

"He really wasn't capable of coherent speech at the time. Mostly just mumbled like the village idiot he is. Jack was carrying him. Apparently Dickwad is making quite the dent in the bar scene these days, and Jack's been watching his back. Which is frightening in and of itself, considering Jack is poised for the Slutman of the Year award."

Drew has been going out. To the bars. With Jack O'Shay. You remember the last time Drew went out with Jack, don't you? Taxi girl?

So this is how it feels to get stabbed with an ice pick—right in the heart.

Billy's voice is sarcastic, drawing her fire away from me. "Hey, Delores, it's good to see you too. I'm great, thanks for asking. The album? Doin' awesome—triple platinum. California? Fabulous, couldn't be happier. Again . . ." He cups his hands around his mouth, megaphone style, ". . . thanks for asking."

Delores's eyes zero in on him, looking him over head to toe. Not happy with what she sees. "It's called a razor; you should get one. If ancient man could figure it out, you've got a slim chance. Oh—and Pearl Jam called. They want their flannel back."

Billy's brows go up. "You're criticizing my style? Really, Cruella? How many puppies had to die so you could wear that coat?"

"Eat shit."

"Cooking again, are you? I thought the health department banned you for life the last time you tried?"

Delores opens her mouth for a rebuttal, but nothing comes out. Her glossy lips stretch slowly into a smile. "I've missed you, Jackass."

Billy winks. "Right back at you, cuz."

He sits in the chair beside me and Delores collapses in the other one. "Okay, Lucy. Fuckin' splain."

I take a big breath. "I'm pregnant."

At first, Delores doesn't say a word. Then she makes the sign of the cross. "The Antichrist has spawned? For fuck's sake, we have to hose you down with holy water or something. Have the Four Horsemen arrived yet?"

Kimberly comes back with a big glass of soda. She puts it down in front of Delores, then scurries away.

Delores takes a long sip. "So you're unexpectedly knocked up—congratulations. Happens to the best of us. What's the problem?"

I stare down at the table. "Drew doesn't want the baby."

As you already know, my best friend is not a fan of Drew's. When it comes to him, she *always* assumes the worst. *Always*. So I expect her to be angry on my behalf. I expect her to go off on a magnificent tirade about man-whores and dogs and venereal diseases. I expect her to join me in another round of the naughty name-calling game.

But she doesn't do any of those things.

Instead—she laughs.

"What are you talking about? Of course he wants the baby. Drew Evans *not* wanting a mini-him running around? That's like saying Matthew doesn't want a blow job when we're stuck in traffic. Just ridiculous."

Needless to say, I'm surprised. "Why do you think that?"

She shrugs. "A conversation we had once. Plus, he and Mackenzie—they're like Master Blaster from *Mad Max Beyond Thunderdome*. Tell me exactly what he said to you. Sometimes guys talk out their asses, and you have to wade through the shit to figure out what they really mean."

"Oh, he was pretty clear. His exact words were 'End it.' And of course the stripper he was making out with at the time really drove the point home," I say bitterly.

Delores points at me. And now she looks pissed. "That, I believe. Fucking prick." She holds her hands up. "But it's okay. Don't panic. I'll take care of everything. We have this new fuel at the lab that's ready for animal testing. He won't know what hit him—I can slip it right through the vents."

She turns to Billy. "You're in charge of the garden hose and duct tape." Then she looks at me. "I'll need your keys and security code."

I shake my head. "Delores, you can't gas Drew to death."

"It might not kill him. If I had to guess, I'd say the odds for survival are fifty-fifty."

"Delores . . ."

"Okay, thirty-seventy. But still, that gives us plausible deniability."

My mother and George walk into the room, interrupting the diabolical plan. My mom hugs Dee Dee tight. "Hi, honey! It's so good to see you. Are you hungry?"

"Starved." She looks at George. "Hey George, how they hanging?"

I think George Reinhart is a little afraid of Delores.

Maybe more than a little.

He adjusts his glasses. "They're . . . hanging well . . . thank you."

My mother coos, "Look at the three of you. Here, all together again, just like old times."

Delores grins. "Frightening, isn't it?"

My mother takes George's hand. "We'll go cook you kids something for lunch."

They leave, and Delores rubs her hands together like the mad scientist she is. "Now, back to the gas chamber . . ."

I cut her off. "Delores—I don't think I'm going to have it."

All traces of humor leave her face. She thinks for a moment. Looks thoughtful, but nonjudgmental. When she speaks, her voice is serious. But kind.

"I'll support you a hundred and fifty percent, Kate; you know that. But because I know you, I'm gonna say this: If you decide to do this? Make sure it's for you—because it's what *you* want to do. If you're doing it because you think it's what Drew wants, or as some warped attempt to work things out with him? Don't. You'll just end up hating yourself for it—and resenting him."

You can't bullshit best friends. And sometimes that's a double-edged sword—because it means they won't let you bullshit yourself.

"I haven't decided anything for sure. Not yet."

Delores's phone goes off in her purse, and the sound of Akon's "Sexy Bitch" fills the air. While she digs into her bag, she asks Billy, "Could you bring my luggage up to Kate's room? I'm gonna crash here tonight."

"Do I look like a fucking bellboy?"

Delores doesn't miss a beat. "No, you look like a homeless person. But I don't have a windshield for you to spit on. So be a good little vagrant and take my bags upstairs—then maybe I'll throw a dollar at you."

With a grin, Billy goes to do it. Still, he complains, "This was *so* much more fun when she wasn't here."

Delores looks at her phone. "Ugg—it's Matthew. I swear, that boy can't take a shit without calling to tell me what color it is." She walks through the back door to take the call outside.

And Billy looks at me. "Okay, I'm a guy—and even I thought that was gross."

Can't say I disagree with him.

A few minutes later, Delores tears back into the room. Still on the phone and going off like a cherry bomb. "Of all the ignorant, balls-out shitty things to say . . . by the time I'm done with you, they're going to have to reinstate your V card, buddy!"

She punches the OFF button on her cell much harder than necessary.

"Problem?"

"Yes. The problem is, people are what's between your legs—

which explains why my husband is behaving like a big, fat, uncircumcised dick!"

I cover my ears. "TMI Delores! T. M. I." There are some things you just don't want to know about your friend's husband. "What happened?"

She huffs and sits down next to me. "Apparently, after I left for the airport this morning, Matthew went to check on Drew. The apartment was locked up like Fort Knox, but Matthew had that extra key. So he goes in and finds your ass-hat ex-boyfriend passed out wasted, on the bathroom floor. *After* he went all Left Eye Lopes, setting shit on fire in the bathtub."

"What!?"

"Exactly. Matthew said if he hadn't gone by when he did, the whole place could've gone up."

I shake my head in disbelief. "What was he burning?"

Delores shrugs. "Matthew didn't say."

Yeah—but I bet it wasn't any of Drew's stuff going up in flames. *Bastard.*

Delores goes on. "So Matthew got the pathetic excuse for a man sobered up. At first Drew didn't want to talk, but Matthew kept at him. And eventually, he spilled like oil in the Gulf."

My stomach clenches, "He . . . he . . . told Matthew about the baby?"

Delores nods. "Matthew said Drew told him everything that went down between you two."

Okay. This is a good thing. If Drew is telling his family I'm pregnant, maybe he's changed his mind. Maybe all he needed was some time to get used to the idea. And Matthew's a great person to talk to in this situation. Not as good as Steven or Alexandra, but still—he's pretty levelheaded. At least compared to Drew.

"What did Matthew say?"

Delores grinds her teeth together. "He said he couldn't believe you would do something like this to Drew."

"*What?*"

Cue the music.

It's the Twilight Zone.

In the end, I knew Team New York would take Drew's side—I said they would. But I thought . . . maybe . . . they'd defend me. Or at the very least, be pissed off about his methods.

Delores puts her hand over mine. "Don't let what Matthew said get to you. It's only natural that he'd back Drew up—just like I'd help you bury the body, even if it was my own dear mother we were tossing into the ground."

"Delores, that's sick."

"Oh, really? You weren't the one who walked into the house and heard her mother knockin' boots with Sheriff Mitchell!"

My mouth drops open.

Delores continues disgustedly, "And they were loud. Like surround-sound, IMAX-theater loud. I'm totally scarred for life."

Let's pause here a moment.

You've never met the good sheriff, so I'll explain. Growing up, Sheriff Ben Mitchell was the thorn in our sides, the rock in our shoes, the pain in our asses. He had nothing better to do than follow us around—breaking up our beer bashes, pulling Billy's car over and searching it for weed.

He always thought we were up to something . . . and . . . well . . . he was right.

But that's beside the point.

Even though Sheriff Mitchell was about the same age as our parents, to us, he always seemed older—like that grumpy neighbor with a cane who never lets you get the baseball that accidentally lands in his yard. Mitchell was never married and didn't date as far as we knew, so it was always assumed that his wrinkly face and piss-poor attitude came from his extreme inability to get laid.

Amelia Warren is the opposite of Mitchell in every way. She's a free spirit. An official card-carrying member of the Healing Power of Crystals Club. A flower child for the modern age.

The very idea of them getting it on is equal parts horrifying and peculiar.

I shudder. "You're right. That is sick."

Billy hops down the stairs. "What's sick?"

Delores drops the bomb. "Amelia and Old Man Mitchell screwing—on the kitchen table."

Billy grimaces. And whines, "Aw, man . . . I ate on that table this morning."

I turn to him. "Did you know about this?"

"I had my suspicions. But I was hoping I was wrong."

Delores agrees, "Weren't we all. I don't know what was worse—having to listen to my mother moaning in ecstasy, or hearing him beg for more and having to visualize what the fuck she was doing to him."

I cover my mouth.

And laugh.

We all do. It starts off small, and then builds—to a table-smacking, eye-tearing, bent-over-at-the-waist crescendo.

"Oh . . . my . . . God!"

And even though Delores is cackling, she insists, "It's not funny! I think my girl parts are broken. Every time I think about it, my vagina clamps down like a littleneck clam fighting to stay closed."

We howl louder. And it's the first real, genuine laughter I've had since this all began. My cheeks hurt and my sides ache—and it feels wonderful.

You know, sometimes I try and picture what my life would be like if Dee Dee wasn't in it. And then I stop.

Because I just really can't imagine it.

Chapter 13

After we got Delores settled in my room, Billy put a call in to his manager. He planned to do a show here at a little bar called Sam's Place, where he used to play in high school. He wanted to honor the place where he came from—give something back to the locals, like Bruce Springsteen always does at the Stone Pony.

And Sam's Place is where we are right now.

It's packed—standing room only. Delores and I are in front, our arms bumping against each other as we dance and sing. Billy's up on stage, a few songs into his first set. He looks fantastic. Dark jeans, a crisp white button-down, and a clean-shaven chin.

He knows just how to work the crowd—when to get them fired up with a guitar-screaming riff or settle them down with soft ballad.

I've never been more proud of him.

The song ends and someone in the back yells that they love him. Billy looks down and laughs, a little bashful. Then he brings his mouth to the microphone. "I love you guys too. So this next song is new. I haven't played it for any of the suits yet, but I wanted to play it for you tonight. It's for someone . . . who believed in me . . . even when there wasn't much of a reason to. And I want her to know that I'll always have her back, that she'll always be in my heart, and she'll never be alone."

His eyes find mine in the crowd. And he winks. I nod, message received. Then he starts to sing.

Years feel like yesterday
And I can't believe how fast time flies
Don't want to let another second go
Without letting you know
What you always should have known
I'll catch you if you stumble
Pick you up if you fall
Hold you when you're hurting
But baby, most of all,
I'll be there . . . so you'll never be alone
Don't ever feel alone

The beat pulses in my stomach. And I listen to the words. And I think about how lucky I am to have all the things I do. Priceless, precious blessings. I have a family that loves me. Friends who would kill for me. Literally.

And I think about who I am. I survived my father's death with my soul intact. I graduated Wharton School at the top of my class. Remember when I first started working at the firm? And Drew Evans was the golden boy? And I put him right in his place— kicked his ass from one end of the office to the other.

I did that.

Because I was stubborn. And smart. And because I believed I was capable. Drew once told me you can change the color of the walls, but the room would still be the same.

And he was right.

I was all those things before him—and I'm still all those things now.

Without him.

From now on, each day that goes by
Gonna give it my best try
To show you what you mean to me
'Cause if I don't have you on my side
None of this means anything
Don't want to let another second go
Without letting you know
What you always should have known

Have you ever lost your keys? And you check all your pockets and pull the cushions off the couch. And then—after searching for ten minutes—you turn around and there they are. On the table. Right in front of you the whole time.

Almost . . . like the answer was too easy to see right away.

That's what this feels like.

Because suddenly I know what I want. I'm confident. Certain. And I know what I'm capable of. It won't be easy—the greatest achievements in life never are. Things like climbing Everest, or becoming the president? They're difficult. But so worth it.

I'll catch you if you stumble
Pick you up if you fall
Hold you when you're hurting

But baby, most of all
I'll be there . . . so you'll never be alone
Don't ever feel alone

I imagine myself a few years from now, walking home on the city streets from the job I love—one hand holding a briefcase, the other holding the small, sweet hand of my little girl or boy.

And I picture us at the dining-room table, working on homework and talking about our day. I see story times, and bedtimes, tickle-times, hugs, and butterfly kisses.

Being a single mother wasn't something I'd ever planned to be . . . but now? It's who I want to be.

I'll be there every step of the way
Won't miss a moment
I'll be there every step of the way
Won't miss a moment

You know that saying? The best-laid plans of mice and men . . . ? You might want to remember that right about now.

Because as soon as the decision takes root in my mind, I feel a dull throbbing. You ladies will know what I'm talking about. That pulling cramp in my lower abdomen. And a thick, warm wetness oozes out from between my legs, seeping into my underwear.

My heartbeat pounds against my chest, and I head for the restrooms. Hoping I'm wrong.

But once I'm in the stall, I see that I'm not.

I stumble back out of the bathroom, into the crowd. My hands shaking with dread, with fear. Because this is wrong.

Wrong, wrong, wrong.

I grab Delores's arm and tell her. But the music's too loud, and she doesn't hear me. I pull her to the back of the bar, where it's quieter, and I force the words out.

"Dee, I'm bleeding."

∞

Forrest Gump had it all wrong. Life isn't like a box of chocolates.

Doctors are.

The vivacious but inexperienced physician right out of medical school, or the battle-hardened know-it-all finishing the last minutes of a twenty-hour shift—you never know what you're gonna get.

"Spontaneous abortion."

My eyes snap away from the gray blob of the ultrasound screen to the steel-blue eyes of the emergency-room doctor. But he's not looking at me—he's too busy writing on his clipboard.

"Wh . . . what did you say?"

"Spontaneous abortion—miscarriage. It's common in the first trimester."

I make an effort to process his words, but I can't quite manage it. "Are you . . . are you saying I'm losing my baby?"

Finally he looks up. "Yes. If you haven't already lost it. This early in gestation, it can be difficult to tell."

As he wipes the cool, clear gel off my abdomen, Delores squeezes my hand. We called my mother on the way to the hospital, but she hasn't gotten here yet.

I swallow hard, but I refuse to give up. Stubborn—remember?

"Is there anything you can do? Hormone therapy or bed rest? I'll do bed rest for the entire nine months if it'll help."

His tone is clipped and impatient. "There's nothing I could pre-scribe that could stop this. And believe me, you wouldn't want me to. Spontaneous abortion is natural selection, the body's way of ter-minating a fetus with some catastrophic deformity that would have prevented it from surviving outside the womb. You're better off."

The room starts to spin as the hits keep on coming. "You need to make a follow-up appointment with your regular gynecologist. When the fetal tissue is expelled, you should scoop it out of the toilet with a strainer. Then put it in a spill-proof container—a jelly jar would work well—so your doctor can analyze the remains and ensure the uterus is empty. If all the uterine matter isn't . . ."

I press the back of my hand against my mouth to keep the bile in. And Delores charges to the rescue. "That's enough. Thank you, Doctor Frankenstein—we've got it from here."

He's offended. "I need to give the patient accurate instructions. If tissue is left inside the uterus it could lead to sepsis, and possibly death. She may need a D&C to prevent infection."

My voice is weak. "What's . . . what's a D&C?"

It sounds familiar. I'm sure at some point in my life I've learned the definition, but I just can't remember.

"Vacuum extraction."

Images pop into my head with his words, and I gag.

He continues, "A suction hose is inserted into the cervix—"

"Jesus Christ, would you stop talking!" Dee Dee shouts. "Can't you see she's upset? Were you in the fucking bathroom when they taught bedside manner in medical school?"

"Excuse me, miss, I don't know who you think you are, but I won't be spoken to—"

Her finger points at the curtained doorway like the snap of a soldier's salute. "Get. Out. She'll make an appointment with her regular doctor. We're done with you."

A slight breeze blows past me, and I'm not sure if it's the doctor. Because my eyes refuse to focus, and my mind is reeling. Trying so hard to grasp this latest turn of events . . . and failing miserably.

Delores puts her hand on my arm and my head turns toward her, surprised.

Like I forgot she was there.

"Kate? We're gonna get you dressed now, okay? I'm going to take you home."

I nod my head numbly. It feels like I'm not even here—like an out-of-body experience. Or a nightmare. Because there's no way this can really be happening.

After everything . . . it's just not possible that this is how it all ends.

Delores dresses me, like I'm a child. Then she helps me off the table. And together we make our way to the car.

꧁꧂

Back in my room, Delores sits at the foot of my bed and my mother tucks the covers in around me. Her eyes shine with unfallen tears.

But not mine. Mine are as dry as the Sahara.

Barren.

My mom brushes my hair back and picks lint off the bed-sheets. "You want something to eat, honey?"

Her voice is a little desperate, grasping for some action that will somehow make this better. I shake my head without a word. Because all the chicken soup in the world isn't going to help me.

Not this time.

She kisses my forehead and leaves the room, closing the door behind her. And Delores and I sit. Silently.

I should feel . . . relieved. I mean, just a short while ago, I thought this was what I wanted, right? Out of my hands.

Problem solved.

But the only thing I feel is . . . regret. Remorse. It fills my lungs and chokes me with every breath I take. Because deep down, under all the fear and the shock and uncertainty, I wanted this baby. I loved this perfect little piece of Drew and me. So much.

I just didn't realize it in time.

Too little, too late. You don't know what you've got until it's gone. All clichés—and all so fucking true. Then a thought comes to me, and I throw the covers back and jump out of bed. I open my drawers and dig through them, searching fruitlessly.

Then I drop to my knees at the closet and drag out the duffel bag I brought from New York. And I rummage through it, like a widow who's lost her wedding ring.

"Katie?"

And then I find it. The tiny T-shirt I bought that night. The one I was going to give to Drew—to announce the big news.

I stare at it and I feel the tears come. I trace my fingers over the letters: FUTURE YANKEES PITCHER. And in my head I see that little boy again. My sweet little boy.

Ours.

The one with his father's eyes and irresistible smile. The one that will never be. I bring the shirt to my face and inhale. And I swear to God it smells like baby powder.

"I'm sorry. I'm so sorry." My shoulders shake and a monsoon pours down from my eyes. My breaths come in gasps, and I clutch the shirt against me—the way a toddler does with his favorite stuffed animal. "Please . . . I didn't mean it. I was just scared . . . I wasn't going to . . ."

I'm not sure who I'm talking to—myself, or my baby, or maybe even God. I just need to say the words, so they'll be out there and real. So the universe will know that this was never how I wanted things to be.

Delores rubs my back, letting me know she's there. That she's behind me, like always. I turn to her. And with my head against her chest, I cry my heart out.

"Oh God, Dee. Please . . ."

"I know, Kate. I know."

There are tears in her voice too. Because that's how real friends are—they share your pain. Your agony is theirs, even if it's not in equal measure.

"It's okay . . . it's gonna be okay," she tries.

I shake my head. "No. It's not. It'll never be okay again."

Delores's arms wrap around me tight, trying so hard to hold me together.

"*Why*? I don't understand. Why did this happen? Drew and I are . . . and now the baby . . . and it was all for nothing. *Nothing*."

I told you I'd be asking why again, remember?

Delores smooths my hair down. And her voice is calm. "I don't know why, Katie. I wish I could tell you . . . but . . . I just don't know."

We stay like that for a while. And eventually, the tears die down. I make my way back to the bed and Delores sits beside me. I look at the little shirt again and shake my head. "It hurts so much. I never knew anything could feel this bad."

"Is there anything you want me to do, Kate?"

My eyes leak quietly. And my voice is frail. "I want Drew. I want him here."

If the world was like it's supposed to be, he'd be here. And he'd be just as devastated as I am. He'd try to hide it, but I'd know. He would climb into this bed with me, and he'd hold me and I would feel safe, and loved . . . and forgiven.

And he'd tell me that this just wasn't the right time. But that if I want a baby, he'll give me a dozen. Drew is really big with the overkill.

And then he'd kiss me. And it would be gentle and sweet. And then he'd say something silly like, "Just think of all the fun we'll have making them." And I'd smile. And it would hurt a tiny bit less.

Just because he was with me.

Delores nods and reaches for the phone. But my hand covers hers—stopping her. Her eyes look at me with understanding, like she already knows what I'm thinking. And she probably does.

"He'll come, Kate. You know he'll come."

I shake my head. "You weren't there, Delores. He was . . . vicious. I've never seen him so angry. It was like . . . like he thought I was picking the baby over him. Like I'd betrayed him."

I close my eyes against the memory. "He'll be happy. He'll be glad the baby's gone . . . and then I'll hate him."

And even after everything that's happened—I'm just not ready to hate Drew Evans.

Delores sighs. And her hand moves away from the phone. "I think you're wrong. I'll be first in line to point out what an idiot Drew can be, but . . . I can't imagine him ever being happy about something that's hurt you. Not like this."

I don't answer her, because the door to my bedroom opens. And Billy walks in. He looks tired, his face is somber, and I know my mother's told him.

"You okay?"

I shake my head.

"Yeah. I figured as much." He sits down in the beanbag chair and rubs his eyes. "This is just . . . totally FUBAR. And when really fucked-up things happen? All you can do is get fucked up right along with it."

That's when I notice the bag he brought with him. It's supermarket brown, and bulging.

He picks it up and dumps some of the contents out. There's a few bags of weed, a carton of Marlboro reds, and two bottles of tequila. I stare at the honey-colored liquid. And I think of Mexican music, and warm skin, and midnight whispers with Drew.

I love you, Kate.

I look away. "I can't drink tequila."

Like Mary Poppins with her bottomless bag, Billy reaches back in and takes out a bottle of Grey Goose.

And I nod slowly. "Vodka works."

Chapter 14

Have you ever licked the floor of the men's room at Yankee Stadium? Neither have I. But now I know just what it tastes like.

Yep—we're hung over. It's hell. Forget the drones; if the army could unleash this feeling? There'd be world peace for all.

I'm in the office of my mother's gynecologist. Billy and Delores came along for moral support. See us there? Lined up in the chairs, like three delinquents waiting outside the principal's office. Delores is wearing sunglasses even though we're inside, reading a pamphlet about the new female Viagra. Billy's asleep, mouth open, head tilted up and resting against the wall behind us. My mother's here too, flipping through a magazine without reading any of the words.

And I just sit, trying too hard not to look at those pictures of newborn babies covering the walls.

Billy lets out a snot-sucking snore, and Delores jabs him in the ribs with her elbow. He wakes up sputtering, "Monkey ball banana blitz!"

We all look at him questioningly.

And he realizes where he is. "Sorry. Nightmare." Then he lays his head back against the wall again, eyes closed. "I feel like gassy stool." Delores and I nod in unison. And Billy solemnly swears, "I'm never drinking again. I'm going legit."

His cousin scoffs, "Heard that before."

"I mean it this time. No more alcohol for me. From here on out, it's weed only."

Yeah. That makes sense.

Since we're waiting anyway, let's take a moment to reflect on one of the most sacred womanly rites of passage: the gynecological exam. It's completely bizarre.

See, our whole young lives, we girls are told to stay pure. Keep our legs crossed, our knees locked. And then we turn eighteen. And we have to go to an office and meet a doctor who, based on statistics, will be a middle-aged man. And then we have to strip bare—completely naked. And let him feel us up. And finger us. *A total frigging stranger*.

Oh—and then there's the best part: the conversation. Yep, he talks to you during the exam. *How's school? Sure is rainy out today, isn't it? Is your mother doing well?* All in the effort to distract you from that fact that he's wrist deep in your vagina.

Can you say awkward?

And don't any of you men out there try and cry me a river about the horrors of your prostate exam. Doesn't compare. One little finger up the ass can actually be rather pleasant. At least you don't have to put your legs up in a contraption that originated as a medieval torture device. Women definitely got the raw end of the deal on this one.

A nurse in blue scrubs calls my name. My mother and I stand up and walk into the first exam room on the left.

I take my clothes off and put on the pink plastic robe, opening in the front, of course.

The better to see you with, Little Red Riding Hood.

I sit on the table, the paper liner crunching beneath me. My mother stands to the side, rubbing my arm supportively. And in walks the doctor.

Take a look. White beard. Chubby cheeks. Round glasses. Give him a red hat, and he could totally ride that last float in the Macy's Thanksgiving Day Parade.

I have to go to third base with Santa Claus? Are you kidding me? Christmas will never be the same.

"Hello, Katherine. I'm Dr. Witherspoon. Your mother's regular physician, Joan Bordello, is on vacation—"

Of course she is.

"—and I'm filling in for her." He looks down at the file in his hand. "Judging by the date of your last menstrual cycle, you're almost six weeks into your first trimester?"

I nod.

"And you've had some bleeding and cramping?"

"That's right."

"Can you describe the blood for me, please? The color? Were there any clots?"

My voice is raspy. "It started out brownish-pink. Like the first day of my period. On the way to the hospital there was a gush . . . of bright-red blood . . . and then . . . it turned brown again. I didn't . . . I don't think there were any clots."

He nods his head, and his eyes are kind. "I've read the emergency room physician's report, but I'd like to take a look myself. Is that all right, Katherine?"

I force a smile. "Okay. And you can call me Kate—everyone does."

"All right, Kate. When you're ready, slide down to the edge of the table and put your feet in the stirrups, please."

While I follow his directions, he wheels a cart over with a monitor and keyboard. And then he picks up a long plastic white wand that looks . . . well . . . like a dildo.

For an elephant.

I lift my head from the table. "Uh . . . what's that?"

"This is an internal ultrasound. Looks a little scary, I know . . ."

No shit, Santa.

". . . but it won't hurt."

And then he takes out a foil packet, tears it open, and rolls an extra-large condom onto the elephant dildo.

Not kidding. I couldn't make this stuff up if I tried.

"Just try and relax, Kate."

Sure. No problem. I'll just pretend I'm at the spa. Having my ovaries massaged.

He inserts the rod carefully. And I flinch. The room is silent as he moves the instrument to and fro. He wasn't lying; it's not painful. Just . . . disconcerting.

"Are you still experiencing any cramping?"

I stare at the beige-tiled ceiling, purposely avoiding the little screen.

"No. Not since last night." I'm pretty sure the alcohol and pot disabled every pain nerve in my body.

I hear the tapping of buttons on the keyboard, and the rod is removed. "You can sit up now, Kate." I do. "Do you see that flickering, right there?"

My gaze settles on the screen, where he's pointing. "Yes."

"That is your baby's heartbeat."

The breath rushes from my lungs. And I'm horrified. "You mean . . . it's still . . . alive?"

"That's right."

My hands squeeze together and I feel the tears coming back up, ready to gush like a weakened dam. "When is it going to . . . How long will it take before . . . I fully miscarry?"

He covers my clasped hands with one of his own. "Based on my examination, your hormone levels, and what you've told me, I see no reason why you should."

My head snaps up. "Wait . . . what? But the doctor last night said—"

"It can be difficult, this early, to detect a fetal heartbeat with a traditional ultrasound. As for your bleeding, some spotting in the first trimester is quite common. Now, however, your cervix is closed, your blood work is unremarkable, and the fetal heart rate is normal. All of these factors indicate a routine pregnancy that should progress to full term."

My mother's arms wrap around my shoulders, relieved and excited. But I need more. "So you're saying . . . I get to keep him? I'm going to have this baby?"

Dr. Witherspoon chuckles.

It's a jolly sound.

"Yes, Kate. I believe you're going to keep this baby. Your due date is October twentieth. Congratulations."

I cover my mouth and the tears flow. I'm smiling so big, my face hurts. And I hug my mother back. "Mom . . ."

She laughs. "I know, honey. I'm so happy for you—I love you so much."

"I love you too."

This is how it should have been the first time. No fear. No doubts. Only elation. Euphoria.

It's the most wonderful moment of my life.

I throw my clothes on faster than a cheating wife caught in the act and burst into the waiting room. Delores and Billy stare at me in surprise. "I'm still pregnant! I'm not having a miscarriage!"

They stand up.

"Holy shit!"

"I knew Dr. Dickhead didn't know his ass from his elbow!"

Smiles and hugs are passed around like acid at Woodstock. And my best friend asks me, "So I guess your mind's made up? You're keeping it?"

My hands drop to my stomach, already imagining the bump. "Until he turns eighteen and goes to college. And even then, I might make him live at home and commute."

She nods, bestowing the coveted Delores Warren seal of approval.

Billy drops to his knees in front of me. "Hey in there. I'm Uncle Billy." Then he looks up at me, worried. "I can be Uncle Billy, right? You gotta let me be Uncle Billy. The only other shot I've got is Delores—and who the hell knows what kind a freak of nature she's gonna squeeze out."

Delores smacks him on the head.

And I laugh. "Yes. You can be Uncle Billy."

"Sweet." His attention reverts to my stomach. "Hey, kid. Don't worry about a thing—I'm gonna tell you everything you need to know. Say it with me: Strat-o-caster."

Delores shakes her head. "It can't understand you, Jackass. It's like the size of a tadpole."

"After last night, it's probably a *wasted* tadpole. But that's cool, right? It'll build up its tolerance—put hair on its chest?"

Delores grins. "What if it's a girl?"

Billy shrugs. "Some guys are into girls with hairy chests. You'd be surprised."

I turn away from the Tweedledum-Tweedledee exchange and walk down the hall to Dr. Witherspoon. My words come out stunted. Guilty. "Excuse me? I'm sorry to bother you . . . but . . . last night . . . I was upset and I . . . drank alcohol and smoked ciga-rettes." I lower my voice. "And marijuana. A *lot*."

A montage of Special Report News flashes through my mind:

Fetal Alcohol Syndrome.

Super-preemies.

Low Birth Weight.

He puts his hand on my shoulder reassuringly. "You're not the first woman to engage in some rather . . . unhealthy behaviors before learning she was pregnant, Kate. Babies in utero are har-dier than you think. They have the ability to overcome momen-tary exposure to drugs and alcohol. So as long as you abstain from these substances from now on, there shouldn't be any last-ing effects."

I throw my arms around his neck, almost knocking him over. "Thank you! Thank you, Dr. Santa—this is the best Christmas present ever!"

I run back to Delores and Billy. "He said it's okay!" We jump up and down in a circle like three kids on the playground doing Ring Around the Rosie.

And it's almost perfect. *Almost.* Because there's something missing.

Someone.

The only other person on earth who's supposed to be as happy as I am at this moment. He should be here. He should be pick-ing me up, spinning me around, and kissing me until I pass out.

And then he should be telling me that of course the baby's fine—because his studly super-sperm is indestructible.

Can't you just see it?

But he's not here. That's just the way it is. I'd like to tell you it doesn't hurt—that I don't miss him—that I don't really care anymore. But that'd be a big fat lie. I love Drew. I can't imagine ever not loving him. And I want to share this with him, more than anything.

But we don't always get everything we want; sometimes we just have to be grateful for what we have. And I am. Grateful, I mean. Happy. Because I'm going to have this baby and take care of him. And I don't have to do it alone. Between my mother and George, Delores and Billy, there won't be any shortage of helping hands. He's going to be loved enough for ten babies.

Forty-eight hours ago, I didn't know what I was capable of, what kind of steel pumps in my veins. Now I do. And I guess that's the moral of the story.

You have to fall down, scrape your palms and knees, before you know you have the ability to pick yourself back up.

So don't worry about me. I'm going to be just fine. Eventually, I'll be great. *We'll* be great.

We pull into the rear parking lot of the diner and my mother rushes in through the back door. She left George manning the ship, and she's a little eager to make sure he hasn't single-handedly sunk it.

As Delores, Billy, and I walk less hurriedly, Delores asks me, "So what's the plan, Stan?"

I breath deep and squint up at the sky. And it feels like a new day. A blank page. A fresh beginning. More clichés, I know.

But still—so true.

"I'm going to hang here another day or so. Just . . . recharge. Then I'm going back to New York. And Drew and I are going to have a long talk. I have some things to say, and he's going to listen—whether he wants to or not."

She taps my shoulder. "That's my girl. Give the bastard hell."

I grin. Billy opens the door for us but I don't follow Dee Dee inside. He asks, "You coming, Katie?"

I hook my thumb over my shoulder. "I'm gonna go take a ride. Clear my head, you know? Tell my mom for me?"

He nods. "Sure. Take your time. We'll be here when you get back."

The door swings closed behind them.

And I walk to my car.

So there it is. You're all caught up now. That's my story. It was a whopper, huh?

My father used to bring me to this playground when I was young. Even then, when it was newly built, it was never very crowded. I don't know why the town chose this location to build; it's an unusual place for a children's park. There aren't any housing developments or apartment complexes nearby. And you can't see it from the main road—it's off the beaten path.

Time hasn't been kind to the metal swing set frames and wavy steel slide. They're rusted, faded, and discolored from the lively primary colors they once were. Still . . . it's kind of beautiful here—in an industrial modern art kind of way. It's solitary. Peaceful.

And I need as much of that as I can get. Because thinking about what comes next, what's ahead of me? I'm not going to lie—it's scary. It feels like . . . moving into a new house. Exciting, but nerve-racking too. Because you don't know where the closest gas station is, or the number of the local fire department. There're so many things to learn.

I read somewhere that babies can actually hear what's going on outside the womb. That they're born knowing the sound of their mother's voice. I like that idea.

I look down at my stomach. "Hey, Tadpole. Sorry about everything that's been going on lately. My life usually isn't this dramatic. Although Drew would probably disagree with me on that. He tends to think I'm quite the drama queen."

Drew. That's gonna be a tough one. Might as well start now—practice makes perfect.

My hand rests against my stomach, cradling it. "Yeah . . . your father. Your dad is like . . . a shooting star. When he's around, every other light in the sky just . . . fades out. Because he's that vibrant—you can't take your eyes off him. At least I never could."

I bite my lip. And watch as a hawk soars overhead.

Then I go on. "We loved each other. No matter what's happened or what will happen from here on out, it's important to me that you know we were in love. Your father made me feel like I was everything that mattered to him. The only thing. And I'll always be grateful to him for that. I hope you get to know him one day. Because he's actually a really . . . great guy." I laugh softly. "When he's not too busy being as ass."

When I finish speaking the air settles, and all is quiet for several minutes. It's so different from the parks in the city, with their honking cars, screaming children, and jogging footsteps. It's serene.

So when a car door suddenly closes nearby, it startles me. My head whips toward the sound.

And standing there is the last person I ever thought I would see out here, in Greenville, at this moment.

It's Drew.

Chapter 15

He looks awful. Stunningly, breathtakingly awful.

His eyes are bloodshot, his face is pale, there's a few days of stubble on his chin—and despite all that, he's still the most beautiful man I've ever seen.

Looking anywhere else just isn't possible.

Drew is staring too. His gaze is unwavering—drinking me in—burning me up.

We stand like that for a minute. And then he walks toward me. His steps are purposeful and focused, like he's marching into a business meeting with his entire career on the line.

He stops just a few feet away.

But it feels like much farther.

And everything I'd planned on saying to him in New York flies right out of my head. So instead, I start off easy. "How did you know I was here?"

"I went to the diner first, saw your mom in the kitchen. She said she didn't know where you were. And she was looking at me like she wanted to chop my dick off and put it on the Specials Menu. So I went out front—ran into Warren. He told me you'd probably be here."

Of course Billy would know where I was. Just like he knew I would want him to send Drew to me.

"Did he do that to your face?" I'm talking about the fist-sized welt on his left cheek. It looks fresh—just starting to bruise.

He touches it gingerly. "No. Delores was with him."

No surprise there. Although I don't think her heart was really in it. If Dee Dee seriously wanted to do Drew damage? She wouldn't have wasted her time with his face—it would have been straight to the crotch.

"What do you want, Drew?"

He lets out a short bark of laughter, but there's no humor behind it. "There's a loaded question." Then he looks off into the horizon. "I didn't think you'd leave New York."

I lift a brow, questioning, "After your little show? What did you think I would do?"

"I thought you'd curse me out, maybe smack me. I thought you'd choose me . . . even if it was just to keep someone else from having me."

Jealousy. Drew's weapon of choice. He used it when he thought I wanted to win Billy back, remember?

"Well, you were wrong."

He nods grimly. "So it seems." His eyes meet mine for a long moment. And his brow wrinkles just a little. "Were you . . . happy . . . with me, Kate? Because I was really happy. And I thought you were too."

I can't help the small smile that comes to my lips. Because I remember. "Yes, I was happy."

"Then tell me why? You owe me that much."

My words come out slow, hushed sadness weighing down every syllable. "I didn't plan it, Drew. You have to know that I didn't mean for it to happen. But it did. And people change. The things we want . . . change. And right now, you and I want two very different things."

He takes a step toward me. "Maybe not."

I'm trying hard not to read into the fact that he's here. I don't want to hope. Because hope really does float, like a piece of wood on a wave. But if it turns out to be unfounded?

It smashes against the rocks—breaking you into a thousand pieces.

"What does that mean?"

His words are careful. Planned. "I'm here to renegotiate the terms of our relationship."

"Renegotiate?"

"I've given it a lot of thought. You went right from Warren to me, jumped in with both feet. You've never just . . . screwed around. Played the field. So . . . if you want to hook up with other people"—his jaw tightens, like the words are trying to stay in, and he has to force them out—"I'm okay with that."

My face pinches with confusion. "You came all this way, to tell me you want us to . . . see other people?"

He swallows hard. "Yeah. You know—as long as I still get to be in the rotation."

Sex has always been a top priority for Drew. That's what this is about, right? He doesn't want the baby—but he doesn't want to stop sleeping with me either? Having his cake and all that. No strings attached.

It's like an episode of *Jerry Springer*.

"How would that work exactly, Drew? A quick fuck on our lunch break? A midnight booty call? No talking allowed—no questions asked?"

He looks ill. "If that's what you want."

And I'm so . . . disappointed. Disgusted.

With him.

"Go home, Drew. You're wasting your time. I have no desire to play the field at this particular point in my life."

That takes him by surprise. "But . . . why not? I thought . . ." He trails off. And then his eyes harden. "Is this about *him*? Are you seriously fucking telling me he means that much to you?"

I don't appreciate his tone. It's derogatory, mocking. Did I say I was a butterfly before? Nope. I'm a fucking lioness.

"He means *everything* to me." I point my finger. "And I won't let you make me feel bad about it."

He flinches, like I've Tasered him with a stun gun. Five thousand volts straight to the chest. But then he recovers. And he folds his arms obstinately. Completely unapologetic. "I don't care. It doesn't frigging matter."

If you fill a tire with too much air, push it past its limit, do you know happens?

It explodes.

"How can you *say* that! What the fuck is *wrong* with you?"

He comes right back at me. "Are you serious? What the hell is wrong with *you*? Are you on drugs? Do you have some split-fucking-personality disorder that I haven't picked up on? Two years, Kate! For two goddamn years I've given you every-thing . . . and you . . . you're just so fucking eager to throw it away!"

"Don't you dare say that! The last two years have meant *every-thing* to me!"

"Then *act* like it! Fucking Christ Almighty!"

"How am I supposed to act, Drew? What do you want from me?"

He yells, "I want any part of you that you're willing to give me!"

We both fall quiet.

Breathing hard.

Staring each other down.

And his voice drops low. Defeated. "I'll take anything, Kate. Just . . . don't tell me it's over. I won't accept that."

I fold my arms across my chest, and sarcasm crackles in the air like static. "You didn't seem to have a problem accepting it when your tongue was down that stripper's throat."

"Hypocrisy really isn't a good look for you, Kate. You gutted me. I think you deserved a taste of your own fucked-up medicine."

You see it all the time. In celebrity magazines, on TV. One minute, couples are all soul mates, never felt this way before, jump up and down on Oprah's couch in love. And the next, they're at each other's throats—dragging out the lawyers to battle over money, or houses . . . or children. I always wondered how that happens.

Take a good look. This is how.

"Well, pat yourself on the back, Drew. You wanted to hurt me? You did. Feel better now?"

"Yeah, I'm thrilled. A regular happy camper. Can't you tell?"

"Can you stop acting like a child for five minutes?"

"Depends. Can you stop acting like a heartless bitch?"

If he was close enough, I'd slap him. "I hate you!"

He smirks coldly. "Consider yourself lucky. I wish I could hate you—I prayed for it. To get you out of my system. But you're still there, under my skin, like some fatal fucking disease."

Have you ever worked on one of those crossword puzzles in the newspaper? And you're determined to finish it—you start off so sure that you can? But then it just gets too hard. Too exhausting. So you give up. You're just . . . done.

I press a hand to my forehead. And even though I try to put up a strong front, my voice comes out small. "I don't want to do this anymore, Drew. I don't want to fight. We can go around and around like this all day, but it's not gonna change a thing. I won't have half a relationship with you. It's nonnegotiable."

"Bullshit! Everything is negotiable. It just depends on how far the parties are willing to bend." And then he's begging. "And I will, Kate— I'll bend. Hate me all you fucking want, but . . . don't . . . leave me."

And he sounds so despondent. Desperate. I have to stop myself from comforting him. From giving in, from saying yes. A few days ago, I would have. I would have jumped at the chance to eat his crumbs. To keep him in my life—any way I could.

But not today.

Because this isn't just about me anymore. "I'm a package deal now. You have to want both of us."

His fists flail in the air, searching for something to hit. "What the fuck are you talking about?" he roars. "It's like I'm stuck in some screwed-up Tim Burton movie, where nothing makes sense! *None* of this makes any fucking sense!"

"I'm talking about the baby! I won't bring a baby into a relationship where he's not wanted! It's not fair. It's not right."

I didn't think it was possible for a person to be any paler than Drew was when he first got here, and still be alive. But I was wrong. Because his face just got whiter. About two shades.

"What baby? What are you . . ." He scrutinizes me, trying to see the answer before he asks, "Are you . . . *pregnant*?"

Kind of makes you wonder just how hard Delores hit him, huh?

"Of course I'm pregnant!"

He takes a step forward. And his face looks like one of those theater masks, horror and hope side by side. "Is it mine?"

I don't answer right away because I'm so surprised by the question.

"Who . . . who else's would it be?"

"Bob's," he says matter-of-factly. Like he actually believes I know what he's talking about.

"Bob?"

"Yes, Kate—Bob. The guy who means everything to you. Obviously you've been fucking him, so how the hell do you know the baby's not his?"

I flip through my mental Rolodex, looking for a Bob, trying to figure out why in God's name Drew thinks I'd be fucking him. "The only Bob I know . . . is Roberta."

That takes the wind right out of his sails. "Who?"

"Roberta Chang. Bobbie—Bob. I went to school with her. She's an ob-gyn. You saw me go into her office the night you followed me. That's how you knew . . ."

His eyes widen, thinking. And then he shakes his head in disbelief.

In denial.

"No. No—I saw you with a guy. You were meeting him. He picked you up and hugged you. He kissed you. He had food."

It takes me a moment to process his words, and then I remember. "Oh—that was Daniel. Roberta's husband. He lived with us in during undergrad too. They just moved to the city a few months ago. I told you about them."

Drew's expression is unreadable. Then he takes a hand and rubs it down his face—hard—like he wants to scrape off skin. "Okay, just . . . go with me here for a second. When you wrote the name Bob in your calendar, you were talking about Roberta, who's a woman and a baby doctor that you went to school with in Philadelphia?"

"Yes."

"And the guy that I saw you with, in the parking lot, is her husband and also an old friend of yours?"

"Yes."

His voice is tight. Strained. "And you think we've been fighting this whole time because . . . ?"

"Because you don't want me to have the baby."

Have you ever seen a skyscraper demolished? I have. It implodes. From the top down, so as not to damage the buildings beside it. And that's exactly what Drew does. Right in front of my eyes. He crumbles.

His legs give out and he falls to his knees. "Oh, God . . . Jesus Christ . . . I can't believe . . . fuck . . . I'm an idiot . . . so fucking stupid . . ."

And I go down with him. "Drew? Are you all right?"

"No . . . no, Kate . . . I'm so far from all right, it's scary."

I grab his hands and his eyes meet mine. And just like that—it all makes sense. Finally.

The things he did.

The things he said.

It all falls into place like the last piece of a mosaic.

"You thought I was having an affair?"

He nods. "Yeah."

The world spins and I'm barely breathing. "How could you *think* that? How could you ever believe I would cheat on you?"

"There was a guy's name in your calendar . . . and you lied . . . and I saw you hugging that man. How could *you* think I wouldn't want a baby? *Our* baby?"

"You told me to have an abortion."

His hands tighten around mine. "I would *never* say that to you."

"You did. You told me to end it."

He shakes his head and groans. "End the *affair,* Kate. Not the baby."

My chin rises defensively. "But I wasn't *having* an affair."

"Well, I didn't fucking know that."

"Well, you fucking *should* have!!"

I tear my hands from his and push him on his shoulders. "God, Drew!" I stand up, needing to get away from him, because it's all too much. "You can't treat people like this! You can't treat *me* like this!"

"Kate, I'm—"

I whirl around and point a finger at him. "If you tell me you're sorry, I will kick your balls up into your eye sockets, I swear to God!"

He closes his mouth. *Smart move.*

I push my hair out of my face. And pace.

Am I supposed to feel better now? Because it really *was* all just a mistake?

If a house gets destroyed by lightning, do you think the owners are cheered by the fact that the lightning didn't *mean* to strike their house?

Of course not.

Because the damage is already done.

"You *ruined* it, Drew. I was so excited to tell you . . . and now whenever I think about it, all I'll remember is how horrible this has all been!" I stop pacing. And my voice trembles. "I *needed* you. When I saw the blood . . . when they told me I was losing the baby . . ."

Drew reaches for me, still on his knees. "Baby, I don't know what you're saying . . ."

"Because you weren't here! If you'd been here then you'd know, but you *weren't!* And . . ." My voice cracks and tears blur my vision. "And you *promised.* You promised you wouldn't do this . . ." I cover my face with my hands, and I cry.

I cry for every second of useless pain. For the crevasse that's still between us—and for the stupid choices that created it. And I don't mean just his. I'm a big girl—I can take my share of the blame.

Drew may have pulled the trigger, but I loaded the gun.

"Kate . . . Kate, please . . ." He holds his hand out to me. "*Please,* Kate."

He looks shattered. And I know, then and there, that I'm not the only one who's suffered.

Still, I shake my head. Because do-overs only exist in playground games. Real life doesn't have take-backs.

"No, Drew." I turn my back on him and walk toward the car. But I only make it a few steps before I pause and look back.

Can you see him?

On his knees, his head in his hands. Like a man waiting for the executioner.

When I think of Drew, two words always stand out: passion and pride. They're ingrained. Who he is. Arguments, work, love— it's all the same to him. Full steam ahead. No hesitation, no holding back. And Drew knows what he's worth. He doesn't settle; he doesn't compromise. He doesn't have to.

"Why are you here?" I whisper, so low I don't know if he'll even hear me.

But his head snaps up. "What do you mean?"

"You thought I cheated on you?"

He grimaces. "Yes."

"You thought I could be in love with someone else?"

He nods.

"But you came . . . for me. Why?"

His eyes drift across my face. It's the way he looks at me in the morning, when he wakes up before I do. It's the way he watches me, when he thinks I'm not looking.

"Because I can't live without you, Kate. I don't even know how to try."

I was in advanced placement English in high school. For weeks, we analyzed *Wuthering Heights* by Emily Brontë. In most of it, Heathcliff is the villain. He's ruthless, often cruel. And as a reader, you're supposed to hate him.

But I never could. Because in spite of all his despicable actions, he loved Cathy so much.

Be with me always—take any form—drive me mad!
Only *do* not leave me in this abyss, where I cannot
find you. . . . I *cannot* live without my life! I *cannot* live
without my soul!

Some of you are going to say that I should've punished Drew more. But he'll do a better job of that than I ever could. Others are going to say that I should've made him work for it more. But we all know that he would have.

And sometimes, forgiveness is selfish. We give it not because it's earned, but because it's what we need. To find peace. To be whole.

I can live without Drew Evans. I know that, now. But if given the choice?

I won't ever want to.

There's only a dozen steps separating us, and I run every one of them. I throw myself at him, and he catches me. He wraps his arms around me and holds me so tight, I can't get air in my lungs.

But it doesn't matter. Because Drew is holding me—who needs to breathe?

"I'm sorry, Kate . . . God, I'm *so* fucking sorry." He sounds forlorn.

And tears well up in my eyes. "I didn't think we'd ever . . . when you said . . ."

"Shh . . . I didn't mean it. I swear on Mackenzie I didn't mean any of it. I never wanted to . . ." He buries his face in my neck, and his regret leaks from his eyes and soaks into my shirt.

I press closer against him. "I know, Drew. I know you didn't."

His hands run through my hair—they caress my face, my arms, my back. "I love you, Kate. I love you so much."

Last year, Drew and I went to Japan. One day we stopped in a bonsai tree shop. They're kind of strange-looking, don't you think? With their stunted trunks and twisted branches. The shop owner told us that it's the knots and twists that make them strong, that keep from splintering even during the harshest storm.

That's what Drew and I are like.

His lips touch my forehead, my cheeks. He holds my face in his hands, and I frame his with mine. And we kiss. Our mouths move in sync—fierce and bruising, tender and slow. And all the rest, every injury, every harsh word, melts away like snow in the sunlight.

They don't matter. Because we're together. We'll find our way.

Drew presses his forehead against mine, then his hand covers my stomach. His touch is reverent and his voice is awed. "Are we really having a baby?"

I laugh, even though the tears are still falling. "Yeah. We are. Do you really want to?"

He wipes the wetness from my cheeks. "With you? Are you

crazy? It's one of the few fantasies I have left. I'd have twenty kids with you—give those freaky Duggar people a run for their money."

I laugh again, and it feels so good. So right. I lay my head on Drew's shoulder. His face rests against my hair, breathing it in.

And then he vows, "It's okay, Kate. We're gonna be okay now."

And I believe him.

Chapter 16

I don't know how long we stay like that, on the ground quietly clinging to each other, but when we rise the sun has moved low in the sky, beginning its descent into dusk. Drew convinces me to leave my car here, that we'll come back for it later. He's worried that I'm too exhausted, too emotional to drive safely. For once, I don't argue with him.

As he drives us back to the diner, he keeps one hand on the steering wheel and one hand on me—my thigh, my shoulder, or softly entwined with my own. And it's reassuring. Wonderful. I'd hoped for this moment, wanted it more than I ever wanted anything else.

To have him here, with me—loving me—after I'd honestly never thought we'd be together like this again.

It's like a movie. The reunion. The reconciliation. The happy ending.

The only problem is, in real life, there's no theme song that plays afterward. No rolling of credits. In real life, you have to deal with what happens after the reunion. The fallout from the things you said, the consequences of the things you did, that almost destroyed it all.

That still could.

That's why we watch movies like that—because real life is just never that easy.

And it's not that I'm not deeply happy in a way I can't fully describe. Despite what I said earlier, there is warm comfort in the knowledge that Drew's words, the stripper, all stemmed from a terrible misunderstanding.

It's the prayer of every person who's ever been told heartbreaking news. Your son was killed in a car accident, you have stage-four cancer. The hope is always that the bearer got it wrong. A misidentification. A misdiagnosis.

A mistake.

But what happens after the "mis"? After you've accepted tragedy as truth, or blown your life savings because you thought you only had weeks to live? What do you do then?

You step forward. You rebuild. You climb your way up from rock bottom with the determination that not only will life go back to normal, but that it will be better, sweeter.

Because hindsight is more than 20/20. Perspective doesn't just change how you look at things, it changes how you feel. And once you think you've lost it all, you value every moment infinitely more.

We pull into the parking lot of the diner and walk through the back door into the kitchen, hand in hand. Like two teenagers who didn't just stay out past curfew, but stayed out all night, scaring everyone who cares about them nearly to death.

My mother stands at the counter, furiously chopping raw carrots with a gleaming knife. It's not difficult to guess she's imagining the carrot is something else entirely. George sits at the small table beside Billy. Dee Dee's on the other side of him, her cell phone at her ear.

When she spots us, she says in a low voice, "They're here. I'll call you back." And ends the call.

My mother's head jerks up. She slaps the knife down and turns to face us. Then she zeroes in on our joined hands and glares at Drew.

"You've got a lot of nerve, showing your face here again."

Drew takes a resigned breath and tries to answer, "Carol—"

My mom cuts him off at the knees. "I don't want to hear it! You don't get to talk." She points at me. "I realize my daughter is a grown woman, but to me? She's my baby. My *only* baby. And what you've put her through is inexcusable."

He tries again. "I understand—"

"I said you don't get to talk! There's nothing you can say that will make this better."

"Kate and I—"

"Shut *up*! When I think about how she looked when she got here . . . What makes you think you can just waltz back into her life, after the things you said to her? After what you did!"

Drew keeps his mouth closed.

And my mother yells, "Well, don't just stand there! Answer me!"

I've always thought of my mother as calm in the face of chaos. Rational. That image is now totally blown.

Drew opens his mouth, but nothing comes out. Instead, he turns his baffled eyes to me. And I come to the rescue. "Mom, it was all a horrible mistake. Drew didn't know about the baby."

"You said you told him about the baby—and his reaction was to hire a cheap stripper!"

And my newly retitled boyfriend thinks it's a good idea to point out, "She wasn't cheap, believe me."

I dig my fingernails into his palm to shut him up.

Then I explain to my mom, "No, he didn't know. He thought I was talking about something else. It was a misunderstanding."

Dee Dee interjects, "Now *there's* a song I've heard before. That tune's starting to get real old."

I roll my eyes. "Not now, Dee."

My mother folds her arms and taps her foot. "I won't have him under my roof, Katherine. He's not welcome here."

And this is why you should never complain to your family about your significant other. They don't know him like you do, and they sure as hell don't love him like you do. So they will never—ever—forgive him like you will.

Even though I can see where my mom is coming from, I've kind of got a lot on my plate at the moment. And she's really not helping the situation.

"If that's the case, then I won't be staying here either."

My mom looks shocked and her arms drop to her sides.

And Delores says, "Hey, Moron—" Drew looks her way. "Yes, you. This is the part where you're supposed to say you don't want to come between Katie and her mother. That you'll go stay at a hotel."

Drew snorts. "Guess I'm not that chivalrous. I'm staying with Kate. Where she goes, I go."

Dee smirks. "Aww, it's like Jack and Rose on the *Titanic*." She raises her hand. "Who else is hoping Douche Bag ends up the same way Jack did?"

I ignore her and stay focused on my mother. Whose voice turns imploring. "It's been an emotional day, Katie. You need space, distance, so you can think clearly."

I shake my head. "No, Mom. I've had all the distance I can stand. Drew wants this baby. He loves me. We need to talk, to work things out." I glance at Dee Dee. "*Without* audience participation."

Then I turn back to my mother. "And this wasn't all his fault. I made mistakes too."

Like many mothers, mine is hesitant to acknowledge her child's shortcomings. "Is that what *he* told you? That this is *your* fault?"

"No, it's what I know. Part of this *is* my fault, Mom." I sigh. "Maybe it'd be best for everyone if Drew and I do go to a hotel."

Stubbornness is apparently hereditary, because then she says, "No. I don't want you at a hotel. If you want him to stay, then I won't object. But I don't like it." She glares at Drew. "You just keep away from me, if you know what's good for you."

Then she stomps out of the room.

George stands up. "I should go talk to her." Before he leaves, he turns to Drew and holds out his hand. "Glad to see you, son."

Drew releases my hand to shake George's, which morphs into a back-slapping man-hug. "Good to know someone is, George."

George smiles and follows after my mother.

Then Billy stands up in front of us.

If you look closely, you can actually see Drew's chest puff out—like an ape in the jungle wild, preparing to fight to the death over the last banana.

"Got something you want to add, Warren?"

Billy looks at Drew. And then dismisses him, turning his gaze toward me.

"I told him you'd be at the park because I knew it was what you would've wanted."

I smile kindly. "It was. And I appreciate that you did. We both do."

I nudge Drew with my elbow. He just shrugs, noncommittedly.

And Billy says, "You don't need him, Katie. It's that simple."

"I love him, Billy. It's that simple."

He holds my gaze another moment, then shakes his head and raises his hands in surrender. "For the record? You two need buckets of therapy, like yesterday. Trust me, I know dysfunctional when I see it."

I nod once. "We'll keep that in mind."

Drew scoffs, "Whatever."

Delores stands up next to Billy and addresses Drew. "I'm gonna enjoy watching you try to claw your way out of the shit-filled septic tank you've dug for yourself. That's going to be better than anything I can think of to do to you." She adds as an afterthought, "And if it's not . . . I'll have to get really creative."

Don't be too disappointed in Dee's lack of retribution. Like the true friend she is, she respects my choices, even if she doesn't agree with them. She knows when to back off and let me handle things.

Or . . . she's just biding her time.

Dee pulls me into a hug and says in my ear, "Don't let him fuck his way out of this one. Multiple orgasms are just a Band-Aid, not a cure."

I chuckle. "Thanks, Dee."

She turns to Billy. "Come on. Let's see if Amelia can stop doing the dirty with Sheriff Mitchell long enough to make us some dinner."

Billy grimaces. "*Way* too soon to joke about that."

They walk out the back door, leaving Drew and me on our own.

I run my hand up his bicep. "George isn't the only one who's glad to see you. In case I didn't say it earlier . . . I'm really happy you're here."

Drew smiles tenderly and touches my cheek. "I know."

We go upstairs to my room, and I close the door behind me. I walk around the bed and slip off my shoes, pushing them under. The shades are drawn, and I turn on the bedside lamp, casting the room in a warm, dim glow.

"It may take some time for my mother to understand everything. She probably won't be very nice to you in the meantime."

Drew sits on the edge of the bed and shrugs. "I'm not concerned about your mother."

"No?"

"She loves you. She'll fall in line when she realizes I'm what you want. That I make you happy. Accomplishing that is really my only concern at the moment."

We're silent for a few seconds. I sit on the bed next to Drew, tucking my feet under my legs. Drew rubs his palms on his thighs. Thinking.

Then he speaks what's obviously on his mind. "So . . . has Warren been here the whole time?"

Although Drew spoke with Billy before he came to find me at the park, I'm guessing his presence didn't fully register until now.

"Billy came home to visit Amelia. He stopped by the restaurant a few days after I came home."

"And you two have been . . . hanging out?"

I know where he's going with this. Like an expert lawyer, setting up his cross-examination with a witness he's trying to trip up. Laying the groundwork, building up to the question that will blow the case wide open.

I look down at my bed, unable to meet Drew's eyes. Feeling guilty, even though technically, I shouldn't.

Drew's habits aren't the only ones that die hard. Like always, procrastination is my friend.

"Is this a conversation you really want to have right now?" I ask him.

He chuckles harshly. "For the record? This isn't a conversation I want to have *ever*. But it's better to get all the shit out of the way now." He shakes his head slightly. "What did you do, Kate?"

My head snaps up. And I feel insulted—defensive—at his implied accusation.

"What did *I* do? You've got some set of balls, asking me that question."

He shrugs. "I think they're pretty impressive, thanks. But my balls aren't the topic of this particular discussion. Did you fuck him?"

"Did you fuck the stripper?"

"I asked you first."

That brings me up short. And I'd probably laugh, if this all wasn't so sad.

In a resigned voice I tell him, "No. No, I did not fuck Billy."

Drew blows out his held breath. And his voice softens. "Me neither. I mean . . . not Warren . . . I didn't fuck the stripper either."

I stand up from the bed. "Did you want to?"

Given Drew's past preference for variety, I think it's a fair question. The way I see it, this was his chance to relive the days when diversity was his norm.

"Not even a little."

He slips a finger into the belt of my jeans and pulls me between his open knees. His hands rest on my hips as he looks up at me. "Do you remember that awful chick flick you made me watch last year? The one with the guy from *The Office*?"

He's talking about *Crazy, Stupid, Love*. I nod.

Drew continues, "And at the end, how he said 'Even when I hated you, I loved you.'"

I nod again.

"It was like that. It was never about what I wanted—it was what I thought I had to do. It was always all about you. You were in my head, in my heart . . . even when you weren't there anymore . . . you were still fucking there."

There's never going to be a good time to say it. Lying or not telling him isn't a possibility.

"Billy and I kissed."

His hands grip my hips tighter. The words hang in the air, like a heavy stench.

When he doesn't respond, I insist, "It didn't mean anything."

Drew smirks bitterly. "Sure, it didn't."

"I was hurt. And confused. It was only a few seconds. And it wasn't about desire or attraction. It was just . . . comfort."

Drew moves me to the side and stands up. Then he starts to pace sharply. Every muscle in his body is drawn tight and contracted. "I told you this would happen. All this time, I fucking told you. That fuckface has just been waiting for the opportunity to sneak his way into your pants again."

"It's not like that, Drew. It was innocent."

The image of Drew's salacious kiss with the stripper slams to the forefront of my thoughts. And my anger is right behind it. "It wasn't anything like what you did. What I had to *watch* you do."

"And that's supposed to make me feel better?"

"I'm not trying to make you feel better! I'm trying to explain what happened. So we can put it behind us and move on. That's what you want, isn't it? *Isn't it?*"

The desperation in my voice must have gotten through to him. Because he stops pacing and looks at me for several moments.

His blue eyes show warring emotions of indignation and begrudging understanding. With the desire to give in to a fury that will serve no purpose—a fury that Drew must know he has no right to feel.

He blows out a breath and sits back on the bed. "Yes, that's what I want."

I smile sadly. "Me too."

He doesn't look at me, but stares straight at my bedroom door. "It was just a kiss?"

"Yes."

"No second base? No sliding into third?"

I roll my eyes. "No."

Tensely, he nods. "Okay . . . okay. That evens things out, I guess." He's quiet for a moment. Then he says firmly, "I don't want you talking to him again. Ever."

"Drew—"

"I mean it, Kate. I don't want him calling the apartment or emailing you. I don't want you meeting him for a goddamn lunch date or girls' night out." His eyes burn into mine as he pleads, "I want Billy Warren out of our life. Permanently."

I close my eyes. Because I knew this was coming. And don't think I don't understand how Drew feels. Maybe you even agree with him.

But choosing between Billy and Drew isn't an option. Maybe it's selfish, but I need them both. Drew is my lover, the love of my life, the father of my child. But Billy is my best friend—right up there with Dee Dee.

"He's my friend." My expression is stoic, telling him without words that I won't give in. Not about this, not this time.

His jaw clenches. "How can you ask me to do this? How can you fucking expect me to see him and watch you talk to him and not obliterate him?"

I take Drew's hands in mine, holding them tight. "If you and I decided to not be together anymore, I still wouldn't be with Billy again. Ever. And he wouldn't want to be with me.

"And when I first came here, I believed you didn't want this baby. And I didn't think I could have it alone. Billy made me see that I could. And more importantly, he helped me realize that I wanted to."

Drew turns away.

I cup his face in my hands and bring him back to me. "If Billy hadn't been here for me, there's an excellent chance I would've had an abortion before you came. Think about that. Think about what we would've lost, Drew. And that I never would have been able to forgive myself—or you. I owe him for that. *We* owe him for that."

He closes his eyes tightly. I don't really expect him to agree with me. It's a hard pill for any man to swallow, especially a man like Drew. But he listened. And I can only hope that he'll think about what I said and realize that my life—our life—is better with a friend like Billy in it.

The fact that he's not actively disagreeing with me is enough for now.

He rubs his eyes wearily with the palms of his hands. When they drop, he asks me a question. And there's despondent curiosity in every syllable. "Why didn't you just tell me, Kate? When you first thought you could be pregnant. Why didn't you say anything?"

It's something you've been wondering about too, isn't it? None of this would've happened if I hadn't kept my suspicions to myself.

"I was . . . stunned. Scared. I didn't even know how I felt about the possibility of being pregnant and . . . I wasn't sure how you would feel about it. I needed time to process it. To accept it. To—eventually—be excited about it. And I was. After my appointment with Bobbie, I was happy. I was coming home to tell you . . . but . . . it was too late."

Drew tells me, "I tried so goddamn hard not to jump to conclusions. Again. When I saw a guy's name in your calendar and then you lied about where you were going . . . I was really pissed. But then I cooled off and I thought, maybe it was good thing. Maybe you were going to buy me something, or plan a surprise."

"And instead of asking me, or waiting to see what the surprise was, you followed me?"

"I couldn't just sit there. I had to do *something*. And then I saw you, in the parking lot, looking so happy to see that son of a bitch. I never thought you'd cheat on me. I didn't want to believe it, but it was right there in front of me."

"My grandmother used to say, 'Don't believe anything you hear, and only half of what you see.' "

Drew snorts. "She was fucking genius."

I'm willing to accept the part I played in the situation, but I don't have a martyr complex. So I ask, "If you thought I was cheating on you, why couldn't you react like a normal guy? Punch a wall or get drunk. Why do you have to come up with these diabolical schemes, like some super-villain from *Batman*?"

He shakes his head and touches my hair. "When I thought I saw what I saw . . . it was a nightmare. It was hell. Nothing God or Satan could ever dream up would come close to feeling as awful as that."

"I can relate."

"And I just wanted it to go away. The fucking crushing pain. Even for a little while. So, after I bought the bottle of Jack, I went to this gentlemen's club me and the guys used to go to in the old days. She was just . . . there. And you know what they say—the best way to get over someone is to get on top of someone else."

"Nobody says that, Drew."

"Well, they should. Anyway, I got the idea that if you saw me with someone else, you'd realize what you were losing. And then you'd . . . stop . . . and come back to me. Plead for mercy. Beg my forgiveness. I had it all planned out."

Dryly, I reply, "Yeah, that worked out well."

"I said it was a plan—I didn't say it was a good plan."

He turns somber. "When you walked out . . . I went a little insane. I just couldn't believe . . . that you didn't pick me." And he sounds so broken, so unlike the man I've lived with for two years.

Guilt- and grief-laden tears fall from my eyes. "I'm sorry."

Drew pulls me into his arms. His lips rest against my neck as he professes, "I'm so sorry, Kate." Then he pulls back and wipes my cheeks. "Please don't cry. I don't want to make you cry ever again."

I sniffle and rub the wetness from my eyes. "That first night, after dinner at your parents', what would you have said if I'd told you then?"

A small smile tugs at his lips as he imagines the wonderful what-if. "I would've gone to the pharmacy, no matter what time it was, and I would've bought one of those home pregnancy tests. Or ten! And I would've sat at the table with you while you drank a gallon of water so we could use every frigging one."

I chuckle tearily, because that sounds about right.

"And when they all came back positive, I would've lined them up and taken a picture with my phone so we could text it to your mom and my parents, Matthew, and Alexandra. And then I would've picked you up and carried you to the bedroom, and I would've spent the next few hours wearing us both out. But it would've been slow, gentle, because I probably would've been worried about hurting you. And then, after, when we were lying there . . . I would've told you I can't wait for the next nine months to go by." His beautiful blue eyes shine with tenderness and passion. "Because I just know we'll make the best kind of babies."

With a laugh, I brush his dark hair off his forehead. Then I lean forward and seal his sweet dream with a kiss.

And he asks me, "If I'd been alone in the apartment that night, what would you have said? How would you have told me?"

My eyes fill up with tears again, and I get up from the bed and take the tiny baby T-shirt from my dresser drawer. I hold it behind my back as I move to stand in front of Drew.

I say softly, "I would've sat you down and told you that when I started working at the firm, I never expected to meet someone like you. And that I never expected to fall in love with you. I *really* never expected you'd love me every bit as much in return. And then I would've said that the greatest things in life are the ones you never expected. And then I would've given you this."

I place the shirt in his hands. He unfolds it slowly, and as he reads the words, his lips curve into an elated, proud smile. His voice is rough with emotion as he says, "That's really, really good."

He sets the shirt aside. Then he pulls the covers back from the bed. He grasps the hem of my shirt and lifts it over my head. Undressing me, baring me to him. My jeans go next, and I stand before him in my beige lace bra and underwear. I unbutton his shirt slowly. My hands skim his shoulders and chest, reacquainting myself with the body I missed so much.

But there's nothing sexual about it. When Drew is clad only in boxers, he turns the lamp off and we climb under the covers. I'm so looking forward to a good, deep sleep. Finally. I see the same weariness in Drew.

Emotional exhaustion can be more draining than any of those sixty-day insanity workout programs.

Drew lies on his back; my head rests against his chest. He kisses the top of my head as he smooths the hair down my back.

My voice is small as I ask, "Do you still think I'm perfect?"

"What do you mean?" he asks in a sleepy voice.

I lift my head to look at him. "You say it all the time. When we're at work, when we're making love—sometimes I don't know if you even realize it. You tell me I'm perfect. After everything now, do you still think that?"

I know I'm actually far from perfect. No one is. But I'm not interested in reality—I just want to know if his opinion of me has changed. If in his eyes, I'm less than I was.

He touches my face, tracing my lips with his thumb. "I still think you're perfect for me. Nothing's ever gonna change that."

I smile and lie back down. Then, with our limbs entwined, we fall asleep.

Chapter 17

When my eyes open the next morning, it's early. Gray light seeps through the curtains, but the sun hasn't risen yet.

And the space beside me is empty. I'm alone.

For one horrible, irrational moment, I think it was all a dream. Drew's coming here to Greenville, our reconciliation—just a vivid delusion brought on by too many Lifetime television miniseries and Julie Garwood romance novels.

Then I see the note on the end table.

Don't panic. Went downstairs to get coffee and breakfast. Be back ASAP. Stay in bed.

Relieved, I turn on my back and close my eyes. I know from experience that if I get up too quickly, the nausea will hit with a vengeance. I don't mind the morning sickness so much anymore. Sure, no one enjoys heaving their intestines out, but in a weird way it's reassuring. Like my body's way of telling me we're A-OK. All systems go.

Ten minutes later, I rise slowly and slip on my robe. Then I make my way downstairs, following the scent of fresh-brewing coffee.

Outside the rear kitchen entrance, I hear Drew's voice. Instead of going in, I peek through the crack near the door hinge. Drew's at the counter, whisking flour in a stainless steel mixing bowl. My mother sits stiffly at the table in the corner. Looking at bills, punishingly pushing the buttons on a large calculator. Her face is stern, angry—hell bent on ignoring the other person in the room.

I listen and watch, catching the end of Drew's story. "And I said 'Two million? I can't bring my client that offer. Come back when you're serious.'"

He glances at my mother, but there's no reaction. He goes back to whisking and says, "It's like I was telling Kate a few weeks ago—some guys need to learn when they're beaten."

My mother slaps a bill on the table and picks up the next one in the pile.

Drew sighs. Then he puts the bowl on the counter and sits down across from my mother. She doesn't acknowledge him at all.

He thinks for a moment, rubbing his knuckles against the scruff of his chin. Then he leans toward my mother and says, "I love your daughter, Carol. Like . . . I'd-take-a-bullet-for-her kind of love."

My mother snorts.

Drew nods. "Yeah, I get it. That probably doesn't mean a whole hell of a lot to you. But . . . it's true. I can't promise that I won't screw up again. But if I do, it won't be as epic as my most recent clusterfuck. And I can promise I'll do everything I can after to make it up to Kate . . . to make it right."

My mother continues to stare at the bill in her hand like it has the cure for cancer on it.

Drew sits back, gazes toward the window, and smiles a little. "When I was a kid, I wanted to be my father. He wore these awesome suits and he went to work at the top of a huge building. And he always had everything together, like the whole world was at his fingertips. When I met Kate . . . no . . . when I realized Kate was it for me, all I wanted to be was the guy who made her happy. Who surprised her, made her smile."

For the first time, my mother looks at Drew. He returns her stare and tells her in a determined voice, "I still want to be that guy, Carol. I still think I can be. And I hope, one day, you'll think that too."

After a moment, Drew stands and goes back to making breakfast at the counter.

I wait, watching, as my mother continues to sit at the table, silent and unmoving. Isn't that what every parent wants to hear? That the singular goal of the person their child loves is to make them happy? I can't believe she's not moved by Drew's words.

She says, "You're doing that wrong."

Drew stops whisking and turns to my mother. "I am?"

She stands and takes the bowl from his hands. "Yes. If you stir too much, the pancakes will be heavy. Too thick. You need to mix it just enough to blend the ingredients." She gives Drew a small smile. But it's enough. "I'll help you."

Slowly, Drew smiles back. "That would be great. Thank you."

Yep—cue the warm and fuzzy. My heart melts just a little. Because every girl wants her mother to see the good in the man she loves.

I breeze into the kitchen. "Morning."

"Morning, honey. How are you feeling?" my mother asks.

"I'm good. Really good."

I walk up to Drew, who kisses me softly and wraps an arm around my shoulders. "What are you doing up? Didn't you get my note?"

"I did. But I wanted to see what you were up to. How's it going?"

He winks. "We're getting there."

We stay in Greenville for another day before taking a late-night flight back to New York. First thing Saturday morning, we step over the threshold together into our apartment.

I glance around the living room as Drew puts our bags in the corner. The apartment is freshly cleaned, sparkling, and smells of lemon-scented furniture polish. It looks exactly the same as when I walked out a week ago. Unchanged.

Practically reading my mind, Drew offers, "I had the cleaning people come by."

I look down the hall toward the bathroom. "And the bonfire?"

We'd talked about Drew's foray into pyromania. He said he'd burned a few pictures, but there are copies. Nothing was lost that can't be replaced.

Kind of poetic, don't you think?

Somberly, I tell him, "Drew, we need to talk."

He regards me cautiously. "No conversation in the history of the world that started with that phrase has ever ended well. Why don't we sit down."

I sit on the couch. He takes the recliner and swivels to face me.

I get right to the point. "I want to move out."

He rolls my words around in his head as I brace myself for the argument that I know is coming.

But he just nods slightly. "You're right."

"I am?"

"Yeah, of course." He looks around the room. "I should have thought of this before. I mean, this is where your worst nightmare came true. Like the *Amityville Horror* house—who the hell would want to live there?"

He's taking this much better than I thought. Until he continues, "My sister has a great real estate agent. I'll call her right away. We can stay at the Waldorf if you want, until we find a new place. In this market, it shouldn't take long."

"No, Drew—I said *I* want to move out. Alone. I want to get my own apartment."

His brow furrows. "Why would want to do that?"

You're probably wondering the same thing. I've been thinking about it, planning it out in my head, since I decided I wanted to keep the baby, with or without Drew. Because there are different kinds of dependence. I've always wanted to be financially secure, and now I am. But I've never been emotionally independent. On my own. And at this point in my life, it's something I want.

If only to prove to myself that I'm capable of it.

"I've never lived by myself. Did you know that?"

Still bewildered, he says, "O-kay?"

"First year of undergrad, I lived in the dorms. Then Dee, Billy, and I and a bunch of other people got a place off campus. After that, it was always me and Billy or me, Dee, and Billy sharing a house or an apartment. And then, I moved in here with you."

Drew leans forward, resting his elbows on his knees. "What's your point, Kate?'

"My point is, I've never not had someone to come home to. I've never decorated or bought a piece of furniture without consulting someone. I'm twenty-seven years old, and I've practically never slept alone."

He opens his mouth to argue, but I go on, "And . . . I think you made a valid point about us rushing into things. We went from a weekend hook-up to living together overnight."

"And look how great that turned out! I know what I want, and I want you. There was no point in waiting, because—"

"But maybe there *would've* been a point in waiting, Drew. Maybe we would've had a stronger foundation to our relationship if we had just . . . dated . . . for a while before moving in together. Maybe, if we had gone slower, none of this would've happened."

He's annoyed. And a little panicked. He's trying to hide it, but it's there.

"You said you forgave me."

"I have. But . . . I haven't forgotten."

He shakes his head. "That's just chick-speak for you're going to hang this shit over my head for the rest of our lives!"

He's got a point. I'd be lying if I said there wasn't a small part of me that wants to drive the point home—that he can't treat me any way he wants to. That there are consequences to his actions.

That if he ever screws up again, I can—and will—leave him.

But it's not *just* about that.

"You want to redecorate?" he asks. "Be my guest. You want to paint the walls pink and put fucking unicorn sheets on the bed? I won't say a word."

Now I'm shaking my head. "I need to know I can do this, Drew. For *me*. And . . . when our son or daughter moves out on their own, I want to know what that feels like, so I can help them."

At this point, I expect Drew to agree to pretty much anything I want him to.

Women know when they have the upper hand. You know what I mean. The days after your husband forgot your anniversary, or your boyfriend spent one too many hours at the bar with his boys watching the game. The days following an argument, when the win is in the female's column, are peaceful. Loving. Men go out of their way to be thoughtful and considerate. They put their shoes in the closet, take out the garbage without being asked, and remember to put the seat up before they pee.

So although I realize Drew's not going to be happy with my reasoning, I imagine he'll still be understanding and helpful.

"Well, that's fucking stupid!"

Not exactly what I'd imagined.

I cross my arms over my chest. "Not to me, it's not."

He jumps to his feet. "Then you're insane!" He pushes a hand through his hair and regains his composure.

When he speaks, his words are calm, reasonable; the level-headed businessman making his pitch. "Okay . . . let's agree the last few days have been pretty emotional. And you're pregnant—you're not thinking clearly. When Alexandra was pregnant she wanted to chop all her hair off, Miley Cyrus style. The hairdresser talked her out of it, and in the end she was glad. So . . . let's put a tack in this idea . . . and revisit it later."

I sigh. "This will be good for us. We'll still see each other every day, but a little time apart, some space . . ."

"You told your mother you didn't need space. That we needed to be frigging together to work through this."

"That was then," I say with a shrug. Then I go for the old reliable, "If you love something, let it go. If it comes back to you, it's yours."

He pinches the bridge of his nose. "So . . . you're going to prove you're never going to leave me . . . by leaving me?"

"No. I'm going to prove I'll never leave you . . . by coming back to you."

Drew pulls the front of his pants away from his waist and looks down. "Nope—still got a dick. Which explains a lot, because your reasoning would only make sense to a woman."

I roll my eyes. And Drew presses on, "You're fucking pregnant, Kate! We're having a baby. Now is not the time to take a step back and figure out if you want to be in a relationship!"

I take his hand and sit him down next to me on the couch. "Do you remember everything you did, before I moved in here? The flowers, the balloons, the Sister B pep talk, the home office overhaul—they were beautiful gestures. Showing me how much you wanted me, and how willing you were to change your life for me."

I look down at our joined hands. "But they also made for an offer I couldn't refuse. No woman could. And I think part of you believes that you manipulated me into moving in with you. That if you hadn't pestered me and laid it on so thick, I never would have chosen you."

"You wouldn't have."

"See what I mean? And that's just not true. It may have taken time for me to trust you again, to believe that you were ready for a relationship, but I would have. I still would have been in love with you and wanted a life with you, because of who you are. Not because of the things you did for me. This will fix that, Drew. So you'll never doubt why I'm with you."

He takes his hand back and rubs it over his face. "So . . . you want to pay for an apartment, pack up all your stuff, buy furniture, go to all the trouble of relocating . . . just to prove to me and to yourself that you can? Knowing that at some point, you're just going to move back in with me anyway?"

"Well, when you put it like that, it sounds ridiculous."

"Yes! Thank you. Take out all the emo psychobabble bullshit and it *is* ridiculous!"

"No—it's not. Because, later, when we decide to live together again, we'll be on equal footing. It won't be you making room in your life for me—it'll be us making a decision together. For all the best reasons."

He looks away toward the door, thinking. Then he turns back to me. "No. I'm sorry, Kate: I want to make you happy, I do. But I can't support something that's so pointless. I won't agree with it. I won't. Just—no."

He crosses his arms and pouts. Like a two-year-old refusing to move until he gets his way.

There was a time, not so long ago, that his refusal would have swayed me. That I would've let his opinion become my opinion. That I would've given in for the sake of our relationship and my sanity.

But not anymore.

I stand up. "I'm doing this, Drew, with or without you. I really hope it can be with you."

Then I walk down the hall to the bedroom.

I stand in the middle of the room for a few minutes, remembering. Some of the most wonderful, and romantic, moments of my life have taken place in this room.

I'd be lying if I said I wasn't going to miss it.

But I'm firm in my belief that my moving out will be good for us. That, at some point, it will make the difference between us crumbling under the weight of our own passion and stubbornness or becoming an even stronger pair than we were before.

I just wish Drew would see it that way.

With a sigh, I move to the closet to get my luggage. I only took one small bag with me when I left a week ago, so there are a lot of clothes to be packed. I spot the large beige leather suitcase on the top shelf.

Walk-in closet shelves really weren't designed with the petite in mind. I stretch on my tippy-toes, trying to grasp the handle. I consider getting a chair from the other room, but I try jumping for it first.

As I bend my knees for my second attempt, I hear Drew come up behind me. He reaches over my head, easily taking hold of the suitcase, and brings it down.

"You shouldn't stretch your arms over your head. It's not good for you . . . for the baby." He walks out of the closet and lays the suitcase on the bed.

"How do you know that?" I ask as I trail behind him.

He shrugs. "When Alexandra was pregnant, I read a lot. I wanted to be prepared in case she went into labor at a family function, or if we got stuck in a cab together during rush-hour traffic."

He unzips the bag and adds, "I would've had to gouge my fucking eyeballs out afterward, of course, but it would've been worth it."

I smile.

He takes me by the shoulders and sits me down on the edge of the bed. "Just . . . put your feet up. Rest."

Then he turns toward the dresser and takes a stack of my T-shirts out of the drawer, placing them neatly in the suitcase. He doesn't look at me as he works.

"You're helping me pack?"

He nods stiffly. "Yep."

"But you still don't want me to move out?"

"Nope."

"And . . . you still think it's a stupid idea?"

"Yep. You don't have many stupid ideas—but even if you did, this would be the dumbest of them all."

He takes another pile from the drawer as I ask, "Then why are you helping me?"

He drops the pile in the bag and makes eye contact. And his face says everything that he's feeling—frustration, resignation . . . devotion.

"In the last two years, I've probably told you a dozen times that I would do anything for you." He shrugs. "It's time I put up or shut up."

And this . . . this is why I love him. I suspect it's why you love him too.

Because despite his faults and flaws, Drew is bold enough to give me everything he's got. To put his heart on the chopping block and hand me the ax.

He'll do things he hates, just because I ask him to. He'll go against his instincts and better judgment, if it's what I need. He puts his well-being, his happiness, second to my own.

I stand up, wrap my arms around his neck, and press my lips to his. A moment later, my feet leave the floor and his hand buries in my hair. His mouth captures my moan as he presses me closer.

I pull back and tell him, "You're amazing."

He gives me a soft smirk. "That is the general consensus."

I smile. "And I love you."

He sets my feet on the floor but keeps his arms around my waist. "Good. Then you're going to let me put three locks on the door of whatever apartment you decide to move into. And a chain. And a dead bolt."

I smile wider. "Okay."

Drew slowly steps forward, backing me up toward the bed.

"And you're not going to bitch when I have a security system installed."

"Wouldn't dream of it."

We take another step together, almost like we're dancing.

"I'm thinking about buying you one of those 'I've fallen and I can't get up' necklaces too."

My eyes squint as I pretend to think about the idea. "We'll talk about it."

"And . . . you're going to let me walk you home from work every night."

"Yes."

The back of my legs make contact with the bed frame.

"I'm also going to come to every doctor's appointment with you."

"I didn't for a second imagine you wouldn't."

Drew cups my face in his hands. "And one day, I'm going to ask you to marry me. And you're going to know it's not because you're pregnant, or because of some misguided attempt to keep you."

Tears spring into my eyes as we gaze at each other.

In a rough voice, he continues, "You're going to know I'm asking because nothing would make me prouder than to be able to say, 'This is my wife, Kate.' And when I do ask, you're going to say yes."

When I nod, one tear trails down my cheek. Drew wipes it away with his thumb as I promise, "It's a sure thing."

And then he's kissing me, with all the passion and desire he's held in check the last two days. Drew cradles my head as we fall on the bed together. Then I arch up, and heat spreads across my stomach and down my thighs as I rub myself against where he's already hard and ready.

Resting his elbows on the bed above my shoulders, Drew lifts his head and pants, "So . . . is this make-up sex . . . or break-up sex? Because I have really fantastic ideas for either one."

I open my legs wider, nestling Drew between them. "It's definitely make-up sex, maybe a little bit of take-a-break sex. And a whole lot of last-day-in-the-apartment sex. That's a lot to cover— so it's going to take a really, really long time."

Drew smiles. And it's his boyish, delighted smile—one of my favorites—that only comes out on very special occasions.

"I *adore* the way you think."

And we don't leave the bed for the rest of the day.

Epilogue

Eight months later

So . . . I've gone back to church. Every week. Sometimes twice a week.

Yeah—it's me, Drew.

Long time no see. Miss me? Judging from the "I'd like to shove your dick in an automatic pencil sharpener" look on your face . . . I'm guessing that's a no.

Still pissed, huh? Can't say I blame you. It was a solid three weeks before I could look at my reflection in the mirror and not want to kick my own ass. In fact, one night I was out with the guys celebrating a massive deal Jack closed, and after one too many shots of Jäger, I begged Matthew to punch me in the nuts as hard as he could.

Because I couldn't stop seeing the look on Kate's face when she walked in the door that horrible night. It replayed in my head over and over, like one of those awful films on cable that's constantly on, but no one ever watches.

Lucky for me, Matthew refused. Even luckier is that fact that Delores wasn't with him, since I'm sure she would've been more than happy to oblige. Yeah—the list of asses I've had to kiss over the last few months is long. Assembly-line worthy. Kate, Delores, Carol, my father, Alexandra . . .

I stocked up on lip balm—didn't want to chafe.

You've missed a lot. I'll try and fill you in.

What do you know about rebuilding years? Every great baseball team has them. Hell, the Yankees have one every other year. The goal of a rebuilding year isn't to win the World Series. It's to develop your strengths, recognize your weaknesses. Make your team solid . . . strong.

That's what those weeks were like for Kate and me after she moved the fuck out. It didn't take her long to find a new apartment. One bedroom, furnished, decent part of town. It was small . . . my sister called it quaint. If I was being objective, I'd say it was pretty nice.

But objectivity's not exactly my strong suit, so it was a dump. I hated it—every square inch.

That first Monday when Kate and I returned to work wasn't pleasant. My father hauled us into his office and sat us both down for The Lecture.

It's a punishing technique he developed during my teen years, when he realized smacking me for my transgressions wasn't as effective as it used to be. The old man's a talker—Wendy Davis has got nothing on him—and he could go on for hours. There were times when I actually would've preferred him to hit me; it would've been so much easier.

The long verbal flogging he employed that particular day with me and Kate involved words like "disappointed" and "bad judgment," "immaturity" and "self-reflection."

In the end, he explained there were two great loves in his life—his family and our firm—and he wouldn't allow one to cannibalize the other. So, if Kate or I ever let our personal lives affect our professional performance again, one or both of us would be looking for a different place of employment.

Overall, I thought it was pretty benevolent of him. If I'd been in his shoes, I would've fired my ass. Afterward, when we told him he was going to be a grandpa for the third time . . . Well, let's just say that news went a long way to mending our fences.

Kate and I saw each other every day, at work and after. There were no sleepovers, but there were dates—dinners, shows, walks in Central Park, marathon telephone conversations that rivaled the yappiest teenaged girl's. We talked a lot. Guess that was kind of the point.

Nothing was off limits. Everything was on the table. We talked about our insecurities—self-doubts are like weeds; if you don't deal with them right away, they multiply. And before you know it, your garden looks like a jungle in Vietnam.

Kate accused me of using sex as a weapon and a security blanket. And I told her she freezes me out—she shuts down, so I have no way to know what she's really thinking. Between the two of us, we had enough issues to fill a whole season of *Dr. Phil.*

Who knew?

Getting it all out in the open helped. I talked so much about my feelings, it's a wonder I didn't sprout tits.

You know when you're cleaning your garage? And you have to gut it—dump out boxes of shit, clear the shelves—before you can put it all back together again? It was a lot like that.

We talked in-depth about what we'd been up to during our hiatus. And let me tell you—those conversations were about as fun as getting a goddamn colonoscopy.

Her tongue-tangle with Warren was dissected in the finest detail.

Was I mad?

Is kerosene fucking flammable?

I wanted to put my hand through the wall—and his face. I still wanted to draw a line in the sand and tell Kate she was never talking to that son of a bitch again. Never seeing him again.

Ever.

But I didn't. Because, as much as I hate to admit it, Douche Bag was there for her when I . . . wasn't. He picked her up after I kicked her in the ribs with a steel-tipped boot. So in a weird, screwed up, the-universe-doesn't-make-any-sense-at-all kind of way, he did me a favor. Plus, the asshole means a lot to Kate. And even though I want to be everything for her, I can't bring myself to deny her something—someone—that makes her happy.

So, in light of my own behavior, I'm willing to give the jerk-off a pass. This time.

Of course, the next time I see him, all bets are off. If Dickweed gets on my nerves, I've got free rein to knock his teeth down his throat. And given his talent for annoyance, it's pretty much guaranteed.

Why are you looking at me like that? Don't tell me you actually *like* the guy now? Jesus Christ, that Kool-Aid must be pretty tasty—everybody's drinking it these days.

Anyway . . . next topic . . . you know I didn't fuck the stripper. But what you don't know is . . . it wasn't for lack of trying.

Before you take my head off, let's keep in mind that Kate had just ripped my heart out with her bare hands. She said she was leaving me, that we were done.

And I believed her.

Which brings me back to my opening statement. That's right—church. The simple fact is, I owe God. Big time. And not for the reasons you're probably thinking.

What do you know about erectile dysfunction? Limp dick syndrome. Failure to launch. It's a condition every poor bastard with a cock is going to have to face at some point in his life. It's horrifying. And like space rocks hitting the earth, it's bound to happen eventually.

But for me, it's only happened once. Want to guess when? That's right—that terrible night. After Kate took off, the stripper did her little show for about fifteen minutes. Then she offered to take things up a notch—for us to get better acquainted on the couch, in the bedroom, from the dining-room chandelier.

But I knew it wasn't going to happen. Couldn't happen. Because I was about as hard as a chewed wad of bubblegum.

Now, maybe I couldn't get it up because I was devastated about Kate. Maybe it was because I'd consumed enough alcohol to kill a horse. But I prefer to think of it as an act of God.

A divine intervention to save me from my own stupidity.

And it worked. Because today, Kate and I are better than ever. And I'm pretty positive that wouldn't be the case if I had actually fucked another woman. I don't know if Kate could've forgiven me for that. I know I wouldn't have been able to forgive myself.

After all that was out of way, we got to the good stuff. The making up. The winning her back. I was always awesome at that part, remember?

But I don't like to repeat myself; it's unimaginative. So this time there was no deluge of flowers. No balloon-filled office. No three-man bands.

There were, however, affectionate text messages. Small but meaningful gifts. Notes on her apartment door. Every time I thought of her when she wasn't there, each time I missed the feeling of her lying beside me, I let her know it. Poetry may or may not have been involved.

And Kate wasn't idle either. Despite her obvious joy over her independent living situation, she made it known she was lonely without me. She insisted we talk on the phone right before bed. More often than not, she'd end up nodding off while I was still on the other end, and I'd spend longer than I care to admit listening to her breathe.

Is that pitiful?

Screw it—I'm way beyond caring.

Kate also cooked dinner for us at her place three nights a week. Then we'd work together at her kitchen table, like two high school honors students cramming for finals.

But around week eight, I felt a grand gesture was called for. And I made my master move.

Have you ever seen *Say Anything*? Remember when John Cusack held that boom box over his head? I took a page from his book. But instead of a CD player, I stood on Kate's sidewalk with a karaoke machine.

You remember how I feel about karaoke, don't you? There're lot of things I do well—singing isn't one of them. But I sucked it up and belted out every pansy-ass love song I could come up with.

Matthew and Steven and Jack showed up and sat on the curb and heckled me, but I didn't give a shit. Because the whole time I was singing, Kate was standing on her balcony, watching me, a small smile on her perfect lips.

And public humiliation goes a long way.

Because halfway through "Mirrors" by Justin Timberlake, Kate came downstairs, took me by the hand, and led me inside her apartment. I flipped the guys the bird on the way in. And once we were there, Kate rode me like a warrior princess charging into battle.

What? You didn't think we weren't having sex, did you? Me, go two months without getting laid?

Why don't you just pull my brain through my nose with a pair of pliers? I'm sure it would be less painful.

We'd been having sex. But like I said before, there were no overnighters. Which was kind of like eating a sundae without sprinkles. It's still good, but there's definitely something missing.

That night, however, changed everything. Because when I opened my eyes, it was morning, and Kate was already awake. Watching me. She traced my chest with her fingers and kissed me. And then she told me she was ready—she wanted us to move in together again.

That . . . was the second best day of my life.

We found a new apartment pretty fast. I'd been looking for a while and had it narrowed down to three choices.

It was important to Kate that we have a place that was "ours" in every sense of the word. For her, it represented a new start to our relationship. A symbol of whatever female empowerment she somehow thought she was lacking before. I'd always thought Kate was strong, independent—I never realized *she* didn't think that.

The building is more than a hundred years old, with original moldings, floor-to-ceiling windows, and two balconies that over-look Central Park. Plus, Bon Jovi lives a few floors below us, which is cool. Kate is a big fan of his.

So, I think that covers it all. Did I leave anything out?

I've learned my lesson. For good this time. Seriously. If I come home and Kate is screwing some random guy in our bed? I won't freak out—I won't say a word.

I'll just pick her up, toss her over my shoulder, and carry her to the nearest DNA lab to make sure it's actually Kate, and not some evil long-lost twin hell-bent on wrecking our lives.

I'll never doubt Kate again. Or us, for that matter.

Still don't believe me?

That's okay. Time will tell. And besides—Kate believes me. And that's all that really fucking matters, isn't it?

Now that you're up to speed, I won't bore you with anymore recaps. But the story's not over yet. You can watch the rest of the action—live.

"I can't eat another bite. I think my stomach's going to rupture."

"God, Matthew—another slice! How can you even?" Delores asks.

Matthew rubs his protruding belly, like a grandpa on Thanks-giving day. "It's a gift."

She rolls her eyes.

The gang's all here. The guys came over to help me arrange the furniture in the nursery, and the girls tagged along to super-vise. Solid cherrywood—that's some heavy shit. Take my advice:

go with imitation wood. It looks just as nice and is a hell of a lot easier to move.

Shamu stares at Matthew as he picks up his fifth slice of pizza. "Seriously, Matthew—you need to stop."

Shamu? Oh, that's Alexandra—new temporary nickname. Matthew and I came up with it a few weeks back when she made the unfortunate choice of wearing a one-piece black-and-white maternity bathing suit to the beach.

Don't tell Steven, though. He's got zero sense of humor when it comes to us ragging on my sister these days.

With his mouth full, Matthew tells her, "Don't be jealous, Sham—just because you're too puffed up to enjoy this fine delicacy."

Uh-oh. Did you catch his slipup?

Alexandra sure did.

"What did you call me?"

"What?"

"Sham. You called me Sham. What the hell does Sham mean, Matthew?"

I've never seen someone lined up before a firing squad, but now I know just what they'd look like. Matthew chokes down his bite like he's swallowing a brick. And his wide eyes turn to me for help.

You're on your own, man. I've got a kid on the way. It'd be nice to have four functioning limbs when he's born.

"I . . . ah . . . I'm coming down with Tourette's."

Delores looks confused. Alexandra's eyes narrow.

"Asslickingturdballmotherfuckerbitch. See?"

Shamu turns away. "Whatever."

Huh. That was disappointing. The pregnancy must be wearing her out. And speaking of pregnancy—Kate waddles into the room.

Her hair is long and shiny. It sways left to right as she moves.

Her brow's wrinkled tiredly, and one hand rests on her lower back to help support the immensity that is her front.

I can't take my eyes off her. She's adorably round. Like one of those Weebles I played with as a kid. She plops down on the couch next to me and puts her swollen Fred Flintstone–like feet on the coffee table.

"I'm so huge."

I smile and put my hand on her firm mound, rubbing it like a bald head for good luck. Knowing there's a real live baby in there, seeing him or her move beneath Kate's skin, is pretty frigging amazing.

When there's a Yankee game on, I talk to it—give him a play-by-play, like a seeing-eye sportscaster. And at night, when Kate is asleep, I balance the TV remote on her stomach just to watch the baby kick it off from the inside. Cool, right? In a weird *Aliens* kind of way, but still cool.

"You really *are* huge," I say. "I think you've doubled in size since breakfast."

The whole room goes eerily silent.

And Kate stares at my hand a second too long. "Excuse me . . . I have to . . . go . . ." She stands up and shuffles as quickly as she can down the hall.

Probably going to piss—she does that a lot lately.

Then Delores slaps me.

Smack.

In the fucking ear. "Ow!" I rub my stinging lobe.

Shamu lets out an exasperated sigh. "Could you give him one from me, Delores? I don't think I can get up."

Smack.

"Jesus! What the fuck?"

Alexandra's all over me. "What are you *thinking*? You don't tell a woman who's three days from her due date that she's huge!"

"I didn't. *She* said it. I just agreed with her."

"Delores."

Smack.

"Christ almighty!"

If the ear-ringing is any indication, there's an excellent chance I've just gone deaf.

"Kate knows I didn't mean it like that."

Delores crosses her arms smugly. "Sure she does, Dipshit. That's why she's in the bathroom crying her eyes out right now."

I swallow hard and look down the hall. It's possible that Delores is just screwing with me. It's her favorite pastime these days, making me feel guilty for all the shit that Kate has already forgiven me for. Delores Warren is the Mickey Mantle of grudge holding.

Alexandra pulls herself from the couch. "And on that note— roll me home, Steven. As fun as it is to watch my little brother grovel, I'm too tired to really enjoy it at the moment."

Delores and Matthew get up to go too, so the four of them can share a cab. Though I really don't know how that's going to work— Alexandra's gonna need the entire backseat for herself.

I'll keep that little observation to myself, however.

Besides, I have more important matters to deal with. Like finding my girlfriend.

⌘

I knock softly at the bathroom door. "Kate?"

There's shuffling behind the door. "I'll be right out."

Shit. Her voice is stuffy. Wet. Delores wasn't screwing with me. I reach up and grab the key from its spot on top of the molding. I unlock the door and open it slowly, and there she is. Standing in front of the mirror, with tear tracks staining her cheeks.

Kate turns to look at me and hiccups. Her tone is pitiful. Sad. "I don't want to be fat."

She covers her face with her hands and sobs into them.

I try to hold in the laugh. Really. But she looks so cute and miserable, I don't quite pull it off. I wrap my arms around her from behind. "You're not fat, Kate."

Her voice is muffled by her hands. "Yes, I am. I couldn't put my shoes on yesterday. Dee Dee had to help me because I couldn't reach."

This time I can't help laughing out loud. I rest my chin on her shoulder and pull her hands down from her face. Our eyes meet in the mirror. "You're pregnant—not fat." I think for a moment and then add matter-of-factly, "Alexandra's fat."

Her damp eyes squint. "She's pregnant."

"Not in her thighs."

Kate shakes her head. "You're so mean."

"I'm not trying to be. I'm just trying to point out the fact that you're gorgeous." I rub my hands up and down her narrow hips. "Sexy as hell."

And I'm not bullshitting her. The midsection might be at maximum capacity, but her legs are slim. Toned. And she's still sporting the sweetest, tightest ass this side of the Hudson River.

Sure, she's hormonal and irrational half the time—but the other half of the time, she's horny. Hornier then I've ever seen her. Plus—there's the boobs. Can't forget them. They're almost as big as her head. So much fun.

Not that there's anything wrong with Kate's everyday breasts—but pregnancy tits are like India. You don't have to stay forever, but it sure is exciting to visit.

Kate doubts my sincerity. "Sexy? Please. Don't blow smoke up my ass, Drew."

I smirk. "Trust me sweetheart—if I'm thinking about slipping something up your ass? It's not gonna be smoke."

She turns in my arms, unconvinced. "How could you ever think this"—she points to her body—"is sexy?"

I hesitate. And rub the back of my neck. "It might make you mad."

"Risk it."

I shrug. "Well . . . I did this to you." A fact I'm sure she won't let me forget, once we're in the delivery room. "I made you like this—left my mark. That's my kid you're incubating. It's like a big neon sign that says PROPERTY OF DREW EVANS. Call me a caveman, but that's a major frigging turn-on for me."

She's quiet for a minute, then looks down at our joined hands. "What if I can't lose the weight after the baby's born?"

"You will."

"But what if I don't?"

I shrug again. "Then I'll become a chubby chaser. A little extra cushion for the pushin' isn't a bad thing."

She rolls her eyes, but then she laughs. I cup her face with both hands and bring her lips to mine. The kiss starts off sweet and tender.

And then it's . . . not.

Her teeth nip at my lips. Hard and urgent. Begging for more. And my legs tremble with the need to please her.

It still amazes me—the power she has. This tiny woman can bring me to my knees with a look . . . a sigh. But I wouldn't have it any other way. I've been to the other side. I've seen what freedom has to offer.

Misery.

Bring on the fucking chains; I'll take slavery any day.

Kate pulls back, eyes closed. Panting. "Drew . . . Drew, I need . . ."

I push the hair back from her face. "What, baby, tell me? What do you need?"

Her eyes open. "Do you want me, Drew?"

I suck on her bottom lip. And hiss, "Yes."

"Show me. Make me feel it. Don't think about the baby . . . just . . . fuck me . . . like before . . ."

Holy Mary Mother of God.

Okay, at the moment, Kate is . . . stretched. Delicate. Like a water balloon that's been filled too much.

I've had to make conscious effort to take it easy with her in the sex department. Slow and gentle, despite some fantastically creative positions. But now, the things she's saying—her voice— Christ, it's all I can do not to bend her over the sink and fuck her till we both go blind.

"I want it hard . . . please, Drew . . . like we used to . . ."

Jesus, this is what a deranged gorilla must feel like, right after he's escaped the zoo.

"Just . . . don't look at me, if . . ."

Like a piece of dried tinder, I snap. I grab her arms tighter than I should and spin her around. My hand tangles in her hair, yanking her head back so I can assault her neck. And my raging hard-on grinds against her ass. Kate moans. My other hand slides up her stomach, gripping her breasts roughly. They overflow in my palm. And our mouths fuse together, tongues plunging, wrestling. I hook an arm under her knees and sweep her up, heading straight for the bedroom.

Kate pushes against my chest. "Wait, Drew—I'm too heavy. You'll hurt yourself."

If I wasn't so aroused, I'd be pretty freaking insulted. I cut her off with another deep kiss. Then I lay her out on the bed.

I take my time opening the buttons on the front of her dress, one by one. Not to tease her—but to show her. "'Don't look at me,' my ass! Looking at you is the best fucking part."

Okay, it's not the *best* part. But it's a really good part.

She wiggles impatiently and I unhook her bra. She slides it off her arms. I take a moment to admire my handiwork, caressing every inch of her bare body with my eyes. *Stunning.*

Then I bury my face between her tits, laving and sucking, giving each bountiful mound its due.

Kate arches her back and pulls at my hair. Writhing. I rip my shirt over my head.

Her arms wrap around my back—kneading—pulling me closer. I moan and nibble a trail up her throat to plant another long kiss on her mouth. I don't want her thinking about the baby right now, but I can't pass by the hump without paying it homage. My lips press against it once, reverently.

Then I stand up. I tear at my belt and slide my pants and boxers to the floor. Kate is breathing fast. Her lips are parted and swollen. And her eyes are on fire—on me.

I grab her ankles and drag her to the edge of the bed, wrapping her legs around my hips.

I slide my cock up and down between her lips, coating the head with her wetness.

Then I stop and our eyes lock. I know she wants a bumpy ride, and I aim to please, but first: "If I hurt you—if you're uncomfortable at all—you have to tell me."

She nods quickly. And it's the only reassurance I need before I slam into her. *Fuck.* We moan together, long and low. My head rolls back and I thrust again.

She's tighter now. I don't know if it's the baby pressing every-thing together or just the fact that God is good, but her cunt grips me like a Venus fucking flytrap savoring its last meal. My hips pound against hers, crashing and rubbing, as rough as I dare.

It feels primitive. Raw. And so exquisitely intense, it could be illegal. Her massive breasts bounce with each push. She's gasping and groaning, loving every second of it. Kate reaches for my hips, but they're too far out of range. She grips the bed sheets instead and mangles them.

Keeping the pace swift and steady, I slide my hand between us and rub her clit, just the way she likes. Then I move higher, pinch-ing those gorgeous dark nipples. Kate's tits have always been a hot spot, but lately they've been extra sensitive.

Her mouth opens, but only small whimpers come out. And that's just unacceptable.

"Come on, baby, you can do better than that."

I give each pointy peak a good, long tug. And she screams, "Drew . . . Drew . . . yes . . ."

So much fucking better.

I move my hands to her knees and hold on for leverage. Pull-ing her toward me as I push forward. Skin slapping skin. "God . . . Kate . . ."

I'm not going to be able to hold out much longer. At this rate I really didn't expect to. My chin drops to my chest and I reach down and grab her ass. Lifting her up—plunging deeper. Moving faster.

Kate's legs tighten on me and I know she's close too. And she's moaning . . . chanting . . . it's a beautiful thing. And then she goes rigid under me. Clenching around me. Taking me down with her. I grip her waist, holding her close as we come together.

Later, when our breaths finally return to normal, I collapse on the bed next to her. "God*damn*. That never gets old."

She laughs. "Yeah. I needed that."

Then she bites her bottom lip and looks at me sideways. Bashfully.

"Want to do it again?"

Like she really needs to ask.

⁂

A few hours later, I wake up from my sex-induced coma to the sound of Kate's voice.

"Ugh . . . goddamn pizza. Damn whoever invented it."

I rub the sleep from my eyes and glance out the window. It's still dark outside, just a couple hours after midnight. Kate is pacing across the room, rubbing her belly. Breathing hard.

"Kate? What's going on?"

She stops in her tracks and looks my way. "Nothing. Go back to sleep." She moans softly. "Just indigestion."

Just indigestion?

Famous last words.

And the next thing you know, Uncle Morty's lying on a slab in the morgue from the massive heart attack he never knew he was having. Not on my watch, buddy.

In a flash, I'm out of bed—sweatpants on. I stand next to Kate, my hand on her shoulder.

"Should we call the doctor?"

"What? No . . . no, I'm sure it's just . . . ugh . . ." She bends over, holding her midsection. "Oh . . . ow . . ."

And a gush of water bursts from between her legs. Like ten gallons' worth.

The two of us just stand there. Stupidly. Watching as droplets fall from the edge of her nightgown onto the rug. And then, like a snake slithering in the grass, reality winds its way through our brains.

"Oh. My. God."

"Holy shit."

Remember that water balloon I mentioned?

Yep—that sucker just popped.

Hee hee.

Whoo whoo.

Hee hee.

Whoo whoo.

When I was sixteen, my school's basketball team was in a dead heat for the State Championship. During the final game we were down by one, with three seconds left on the clock. Guess who they passed the ball to? Who sank the winning three-pointer?

Yep—that would be me. Because even back then, I was a rock. Steady on the draw. I don't get stressed. Fear? Panic? They're for losers.

And I'm no loser.

So why are my hands shaking like an unmedicated Parkinson's patient?

Anyone ever tell you, you ask too many frigging questions?

My knuckles are white, wrapped in a death grip around the steering wheel.

Kate is in the passenger seat—with a towel under her ass—implementing every breathing technique those wacked-out hippie Lamaze instructors told us about.

Hee hee.

Whoo whoo.

Hee hee.

Whoo.

Then, mid-whoo, she screams. "Oh, no!"

I almost slam the car into a goddamn telephone pole. "What! What's wrong?"

"I forgot the sour apple lollipops!"

"The *what?*"

Her voice is heavy with disappointment. "The sour apple lollipops. Alexandra said they were the only thing that quenched her thirst when she was in labor with Mackenzie. I was going to pick some up this afternoon, but I forgot. Can we stop and get some?"

Okay. It seems that Kate's common sense has gone bye-bye—so it's up to me to be the voice of reason. Which is pretty frigging frightening, considering I'm hanging on by a thread over here.

"No, we can't fucking stop and get some! Are you out of your mind?"

Kate's big brown eyes immediately fill with tears. And I feel like the world's biggest dick.

"Please, Drew? I just want everything to be perfect . . . and what if I want a lollipop during the delivery, and you go to get me one, and then I have the baby while you're gone? You'll miss it." Tears course down her cheeks like two little tributaries. "I couldn't *bear* it if you missed it."

Please don't let it be a girl. For God's sake, please don't let it be a girl. All this time, I've been praying for a healthy baby without specifying a sex.

Until now.

Because if I have a daughter, and her tears cut me off at the knees like Kate's do? I'm totally fucking screwed.

"Okay, Kate. It's all right, baby. Don't cry—I'll stop."

She sniffles. And smiles. "Thank you."

I jerk the wheel to the right, make an illegal U-turn, and pull onto the curb in front of a 7-Eleven. Then, faster than a pit stop at the Indy 500, I'm back on the road, with the coveted sour apple lollipops rolling around in the backseat.

And Kate is back to her breathing.

Hee hee.

Whoo whoo.

Hee hee.

Until she's not.

"Do you think the nurses will know we had sex?"

I look pointedly at her stomach. "Unless you plan on claiming an immaculate conception, I think they'll have a pretty good idea."

Then I lean on the horn. "The gas is the one on the right, grandma!" I swear to Christ, if your gray poufy hair is the only thing that can see over the dashboard? You've got no business driving.

Hee hee.

Whoo whoo.

"No—do you think they'll know we had sex tonight?"

Kate is funny about things like this. Shy. Even with me sometimes. The other day, I happened to catch a passing glimpse of her sitting on the toilet and it was like the end of the world. Personally, I think it's ridiculous. But I'm not about to argue the point with her now.

"It's a maternity ward, Kate, not CSI. They're not gonna to be down there with a black light looking for my swimmers."

Hee Hee.

Hee Hee.

"Yeah, you're right. They won't be able to tell." She seems calmed by the idea. Reassured.

Whooooo.

And I'm happy for her. Now if I can just keep myself from going into cardiac arrest, we'll be in pretty good shape.

An hour later, Kate is settled into a private room at New York Pres-byterian, hooked up to more beeping contraptions then a ninety-year-old on life support. I sit down in the chair next to the bed. "Can I get you anything? Back rub? Ice chips? Narcotics?"

I know I could go for a glass of whiskey at the moment. Or a whole bottle.

Kate takes my hand and holds it tight, like we're on a plane that's about to take off. "No. Just—talk to me." Then her voice turns hushed. Small. "I'm scared, Drew."

My chest tightens painfully. And I've never felt so helpless in my life.

But I do my damnedest to hide it. "Hey, this whole delivery thing is a piece of cake. I mean, women have babies all the time. I read this article once that said in the olden days, they'd pop a kid out right in the middle of the fields. Then they'd clean it off, put it in their backpack, and go right back to work. How hard can it be?"

She snorts. "Easy for you to say. Your part was fun. And over. Females got royally screwed in this deal."

She's not wrong. But women are stronger than men. No, really, I'm being serious. Sure, we can outdo them in upper-body strength, but in every other way—psychologically, emotionally, cardiovascu-larly, genetically—women come out on top.

"That's because God is wise. He knew if we had to go through this shit, the human race would've died the fuck out with Adam."

She chuckles.

Then a voice comes from the doorway. "How are we doing this evening?"

"Hi, Bobbie."

"Hey, Roberta."

Yes—I only use her full name. Post-traumatic stress? Possibly. All I know is that hearing the name Bob? Pretty much makes me want to slit my wrists open with a box cutter.

Roberta checks the chart at the end of the bed. "Everything looks good. You're about three centimeters dilated, Kate, so we've still got a while to go. Do you have any questions for me?"

Kate looks hopeful. "Epidural?"

Here's some advice—don't be a masochist. Get the epidural.

I'll repeat that in case you missed it: GET THE EPIDURAL.

According to my sister, it's a miracle drug. She'd gladly jerk off the guy who invented it—and Steven would probably let her. Would you get a tooth pulled without novocaine? Would you get your appendix removed without anesthesia? Of course not.

And don't give me that bullshit about having the "full experience" of childbirth. Pain is pain—there's nothing "wondrous" about it.

It just fucking hurts.

Roberta smiles soothingly. "I'll get it set up right away." She makes a few notes on the clipboard, then returns it to its hanging place. "I'll come back in a little while to check on you. Have the nurses page me if you need anything."

"Okay. Thanks, Roberta."

Once she's out the door, I stand up and grab my cell phone.

"I'm going to go call your mom—I can't get any reception in here. Will you be all right till I get back?"

She waves her hand. "Sure. Not going anywhere. We'll be right here."

I bend over and kiss Kate's forehead. Then I lean down and kiss the hump, telling it, "Don't start without me."

Then I'm out the door—jogging to catch up with Kate's doctor down the hall. "Hey, Roberta!"

She stops and turns. "Hi, Drew. How are you?"

"I'm good—good. I wanted to ask you about the baby's heart rate. Isn't one-fifty a little high?"

Roberta's voice is tolerant, understanding. She's used to this by now.

"It's well within the normal range. It's common to see some minor fluctuations in the fetal heart rate during labor."

I nod. And go on. "And Kate's blood pressure? Any sign of preeclampsia?"

Knowledge is power. The more you know, the more control you have over a situation. At least that's what I've been telling myself for the last eight months.

"No, like I told you on the phone yesterday—and the day before that—Kate's blood pressure is perfect. It's been steady the entire pregnancy."

I rub my chin and nod. "Have you ever actually delivered a baby with shoulder dystocia? Because you realize you won't know it's happening until the baby's head is already—"

"Drew. I thought we agreed you were going to stop watching *ER* reruns?"

ER should come with a warning label. It's disturbing. If you're a mild hypochondriac or a parent to be, expect to lose a shitload of sleep after just one episode.

"I know, but—"

Roberta puts her hand up. "Look, I know how you feel—"

"Do you?" I ask sharply. "Have you ever taken your whole life and put it in someone else's hands and asked them to take care of it for you? To bring it back to you in one piece? 'Cause that's what I'm doing here." I push a hand through my hair and look away. And when I speak again, my voice is shaky. "Kate and this baby . . . if anything ever . . ."

I can't even finish the thought, let alone the sentence.

She puts her hand on my shoulder. "Drew, you have to trust me. I know it's difficult, but try and focus on the positives. Kate is young and healthy—we have every reason to believe that this delivery will progress without any complications at all."

I nod my head. And the logical part of my brain knows she's right.

"Go back to Kate. Try and enjoy the time you have left. After tonight, it's not going to be just the two of you anymore—not for a long time."

I force myself to nod again. "Okay. Thanks."

I turn and walk back toward the room. I stop in the doorway. Can you see her?

Surrounded by pillows—buried under the puffy down comforter she insisted on bringing from home. She looks so tiny. Almost like a little girl hiding in her parents' bed during a thunderstorm.

And I need to say the words—to make sure she knows.

"I love you, Kate. Everything that's good in my life, anything that really matters, is only there because of you. If we hadn't met? I'd be fucking miserable—and probably too clueless to even realize it."

She looks at me, totally straight faced. "I'm having a baby, Drew—I'm not dying." Then her eyes widen. "Jesus Christ, I'm not dying, am I?"

And that's all it takes to snap me out of my panic.

"No, Kate. You're not dying."

She nods. "Okay, then. And just for the record, I love you too. I love that you're funding Mackenzie's future because you won't stop cursing. I love how you tease your sister unmercifully but would kill anyone who hurt her. But most of all . . . I love how you love me. I feel it every moment . . . every day."

I walk up to her and cup her cheek. Then I lean over and softly kiss her lips.

She takes my hand and gives it a squeeze. And then her jaw tightens with determination.

"Now, let's do this thing."

⟡

Turns out all the worrying was for nothing. Because at 9:57 this morning, Kate gave birth to a bouncing baby boy. And I was right next to her the whole time. Sharing her pain.

Literally.

I'm pretty sure she broke my hand.

But who cares? A few broken bones don't mean much—not when you're holding a seven-pound, nine-ounce miracle.

And that's just what I'm doing.

I know every parent thinks their child is adorable—but be honest—he's one good-looking kid, don't you think? A patch of black hair lays smoothly on top of his head. His hands, his nose, his lips—looking at them is like looking in a mirror. But his eyes, they're all Kate.

He's exquisite. Perfection made flesh.

Granted, he didn't come out looking like this. A few hours ago, he bore a strong resemblance to a screaming featherless chicken.

But he was *my* screaming featherless chicken, so he was still the most beautiful fucking thing I've ever seen.

It's unreal. The adoration. The worship that's so overwhelming, it almost hurts to look at him. I mean, I love Kate—more than my own life. But that took time. I *gradually* fell in love with her.

This . . . was instantaneous. As soon as I laid eyes on him, I knew I'd gladly jump bare-assed into a pool of battery acid for him. Insane, right? And I can't wait to teach him things. Show him . . . everything. Like how to change a tire, and sweet talk a girl, how to hit a baseball, and throw a right hook. Not necessarily in that order.

I used to make fun of those guys at the park. The dads with their strollers and goofy smiles and man purses.

But now . . . now I get it.

Kate's voice pulls me from my baby gazing. "Hey."

She sounds worn out. I don't blame her.

"How are you feeling?"

She smiles sleepily. "Well . . . imagine peeing out a watermelon. "

I flinch. "Ouch."

"Yeah."

Her eyes fall to the pale-blue-blanketed bundle in my arms. "How's the little guy?"

"He's good. We're just hanging out. Shooting the shit. I'm telling him about all the important things in life, like chicks and cars and . . . chicks."

"Is that so?"

"Yep."

I look down at our son. And my voice is awed. "You did such

a great job, Kate. He has your eyes. I love your eyes—did I ever tell you that? They were the first thing I noticed about you."

She cocks one brow. "I thought my ass was the first thing you noticed?"

I laugh, remembering. "Oh yeah, that's right. But then you turned around and just . . . blew me away."

The baby lets out a sharp squawk, capturing our attention.

"I think he's hungry."

Kate nods and I pass him over. She undoes the clasp of her pajama top, exposing one ripe, juicy breast. She brings the baby close and he latches onto her nipple—like an expert.

Did you expect anything less? This is my son, after all.

I watch them for a moment. Then I have to reach down to adjust the tent pole that's sprung up in my pants.

Sick. Yeah—I know.

Kate throws me a smirk and glances toward my crotch. "Got a problem down there, Mr. Evans?"

I shrug. "Nope. No problem. Just looking forward to my turn."

See—there're two kinds of women in this world: The ones who figure if they can't get any below-the-waist action for six weeks after giving birth, neither can their guy. Then there's the second group. The ones who look forward to those hand jobs, blow jobs, and then some—because they know the favor will be returned when the ban is lifted.

Kate definitely falls into the second group. I know this, and apparently so does my cock.

"After the massacre you witnessed in the delivery room? I didn't think you'd ever want to have sex with me again."

My mouth falls open. In shock.

"Are you frigging kidding me? I mean, I thought your cunt was magnificent before, but now that I've see what it's really capable of?

It's reached superhero status in my book. In fact, I think that's what we should name it." I lift my hands, envisioning a giant billboard. "Incred-a-Pussy."

She shakes her head. And smiles down at the baby. "Speaking of naming things . . . we should probably come up with one for him, don't you think?"

Kate and I decided to wait on the name game until after the baby was born—to make sure it was a good fit. Names are crucial. They're the first impression the world has of you. That's why I'll never understand why people curse their kids with labels like Edmund, or Albert, or Morning Dew.

Why don't you just cut to the chase and call the kid Shit Head?

I lean back in the chair. "Okay—you can start first."

Her eyes roam the baby's face. "Connor."

I shake my head. "Connor's not a first name."

"Of course it is."

"No—it's a last name." In my best Terminator voice I say, "Sarah Connor."

Kate rolls her eyes. Then she says, "I've always liked the name Dalton."

"I'm not even going to dignify that with a response."

"O-kay. Colin."

I scoff, "No way. Sounds too much like 'colon.' They'll be calling him Asshole the minute he steps foot on the playground."

Kate looks at me incredulously. "Are you sure you went to Catholic school? It sounds like you grew up in juvie hall."

Life is one big school playground. Remember that.

Wolf-pack mentality. You need to learn early how not to be the weakest link. They're the ones who get eaten. Alive.

"Since you don't approve of my choices, what do you suggest?" she asks.

I look at the sleeping face of our son. His perfect little lips, his long dark lashes.

"Michael."

"Uh-uh. In third grade, Michael Rollins threw up all over my penny loafers. Whenever I hear that name I think of regurgitated hot dogs."

Fair enough. I try again. "James. Not Jim or Jimmy—and sure as shit not Jamie. Just James."

Kate raises her eyebrows. And tests it out. "James. James—I like it."

"Yeah?"

She looks down at the baby again. "Yes. James it is."

I reach into my back pocket and pull out a folded piece of paper. "Fantastic. Now for his last name."

She's confused. "His last name?"

We've talked about using Brooks as the middle name. But let's be honest—the only people who use a middle name are serial killers and pissed-off parents. So I came up with something much better.

I put the opened paper on Kate's lap.

Take a look.

BROOKS-EVANS

She looks up, eyes wide with surprise. "You want to hyphenate his name?"

I'm an old-fashioned kind of guy. I think women should take their husband's last names. Sure, it comes from the idea that a woman is property. And no, I don't agree with that. In the future, if some punk comes along and implies that he *owns* my niece—I'm gonna buy him a shovel.

So he can dig his own grave before I put him in it.

But technically speaking, Kate is the last of the Brookses. Namesakes don't mean as much anymore, but I have a feeling it means a lot to her.

"Well . . . he's ours. And you did do most of the work. You should share half the credit."

Her eyes soften as she reminds me, "You hate to share, Drew."

I push some wayward hair behind her ear. "For you, I'm willing to make an exception."

Plus, I'm banking on the fact that one day soon, Kate's last name will match our son's.

Of course, Kate deserves the best proposal ever—and the best takes time.

Planning.

It's in the works right now. I'm taking ballooning lessons on Saturday afternoons, when she thinks I'm playing ball with the guys. Because I'm going to take Kate on a private hot-air balloon ride to the Hudson Valley. There'll be an elegant picnic ready for us when we land. And that's where I'll pop the question

That way—on the outside chance Kate actually turns me down—I'll have her in a totally secluded area until I can change her mind.

Genius, right?

I'll have a limo waiting nearby—but not too near—to drive us back home, so we can sit back and relax on the way. And have limo sex, of course. You should never pass up the opportunity to have sex in a limo—it's always fun.

Kate's eyes are shiny with tears. Happy ones. "I love it. James Brooks-Evans. It's perfect. Thank you."

I lean forward and kiss our son's forehead. And then I kiss his mother's lips. "You've got it all wrong, baby. I'm supposed to be thanking you."

She looks down at James tenderly. And in that voice that could make an angel green with envy, she starts to sing.

There's a song that they sing when they take to the highway
A song that they sing when they take to the sea
A song that they sing of their home in the sky
Maybe you can believe it if it helps you to sleep
But singing works just fine for me
So good night you moonlight ladies
Rock-a-bye sweet baby James
Deep greens and blues are the colors I choose
Won't you let me go down in my dreams
And rock-a-bye sweet baby James

There's only a few times in a guy's life that he's allowed to cry without looking like a total chump.

This is one of those times.

When Kate is finished, I clear my throat. And rub the wetness from my eyes. Then I climb onto the bed beside her.

I'm pretty sure it's against hospital policy, and I admit, some of those male nurses look pretty fucking intimidating.

But come on—they're *nurses*.

Kate turns toward me, so James lies between us. My arm lays over him, my hand on her hip, encircling them both.

Kate's eyes are velvety warm. "Drew?"

"Mmm?"

"Do you think we'll always be like this?"

I give her a small smile. "Definitely not."

And then I touch her face—the one I plan on looking at every morning and every night, until death shows up to drag me away.

"We're just gonna keep getting better."

So there you have it.

How's that for a happy frigging ending, huh? Or beginning . . . I guess . . . depending on how you look at it.

Anyway, now's about the time I start spouting off some pearls of wisdom.

Advice.

But given the events of the last year, it's become increasingly obvious that I don't know what the fuck I'm talking about. I don't think you should listen to anything I've said.

You still want me to give it a shot?

Okay. But don't say I didn't warn you.

Here goes:

Number One—people don't change. There's no magic bullet. No bibbety-fucking-boo.

What you see is what you get. Sure, certain habits can be tweaked. Reined in. Like my propensity for making snap judgments. The very idea of assuming I know everything—without checking with Kate first—now makes me sick to my stomach.

But other characteristics, they stick.

My possessiveness, Kate's stubbornness, our collective competitiveness—they're too much a part of who we are to be totally eradicated.

It's kind of like . . . cellulite. You ladies can spend all day at the spa wrapped in mud and seaweed. You can throw a fortune away on those ridiculous creams and scrubs. But at the end of the day, that puckered, dimply skin is still gonna be there.

Sorry to be the one to break it to you; it's just the way it is.

But if you love someone, *really* love them, you take them as is. You don't try to change them.

You want the whole package—cottage cheese ass and all.

Number Two—life isn't perfect. Or predictable. Don't expect it to be.

One minute, you're swimming along in the ocean. The water's smooth and calm; you're relaxed. And then—out of nowhere—an undertow sucks you down.

It's what you do next that counts. Do you give it all you've got? Kick for the surface, even though your arms and legs are aching? Or do you give up and let yourself drown?

How you react to life's twists and turns makes all the difference.

So Number Three—the important thing is, if you can make it through the rough, unexpected times? That light at the end of the tunnel is worth all the shit you had to wade through to get there.

That's something I'll never forget. I'm reminded of it every time I look at Kate. Every time I look at our son.

When it's all said and done? The payoff is way more than fucking worth it.

Turn the page for a sneak peek

at how Kate and Drew's best friends

handle falling in love

in Emma Chase's next book

Tamed

COMING SOON FROM GALLERY BOOKS

I pull on a pair of silk boxers then heat up a bowl of leftover pasta and chicken. I'm not Italian, but I'd eat this every day of the week if I could. It's about eight thirty by the time I finish washing the dishes. Yes, I am man who washes his own dishes.

Be jealous, ladies—I'm a rare breed.

Then I flop back on my awesome, king-size bed and grab the golden ticket from the pocket of my discarded pants.

I finger the letters on the bright green cardstock.

DEE WARREN

CHEMIST

LINTRUM FUELS

And I remember the soft, smooth flesh that swelled from the confines of her tight, pink shirt. My dick twitches—guess he remembers it too.

Normally I'd wait a day or two to call a girl like Delores. Timing is everything. Looking too eager is a rookie mistake—women enjoy being panted after by puppies, not men.

But it's already Wednesday night, and I'm hoping to meet up with Dee on Friday. The twenty-first century is the age of *Maybe He's Just Not That Into You* and *Dating for Dummies* and *The Girlfriends' Guide to Dating,* which means calling a chick for a random hookup isn't as easy as it used to be. There are all these frigging rules now—I found that out the hard way.

Like if a guy wants to meet up with you the same night that he calls, you're supposed to say "no," because that means he doesn't respect you. And, if he wants to take you out on a Tuesday, that's a sign he's got better plans for Saturday night.

Trying to keep up with the changing edicts is tougher than keeping track of the goddamn health care debate in Congress. It's like a minefield—one wrong step and your cock won't be getting any action for a long time. But, if getting laid were easy, everyone would be doing it. It . . . and pretty much nothing else.

Which brings me to my next thought: I know feminists always complain about how men have all the power. But when it comes to dating—in America, at least? That's not really the case. In the bars, on the weekends, it's ladies' choice 24/7. They have their pick of the litter because single men will never reject a come-on.

Picture it: The music's pumping, bodies are grinding, and a non-hideous female approaches a dude having a drink at the bar. She says, "I want to fuck your brains out." He replies, "Nah, I'm not really in the mood for sex tonight." SAID NO MAN *EVER*.

Chicks never have to worry about getting shot down—as long as they're not shooting too far above their pay grade. They never have to stress about when they're going to get lucky. For women, sex is an all-you-can-eat buffet—they just have to choose a dish. God created men with a strong sex drive to ensure the survival of the species. Be fruitful and multiply and all that. For guys like me, who know what the fuck they're doing, it's not exactly difficult. But for my not-as-skilled brethren, getting some can be a daunting task.

A slight buzz of adrenaline rushes through me as I pick up the phone to dial the cell number on the business card. It's not that I feel nervous, more like . . . cautious anticipation. My hand taps my leg in time to "Enter Sandman" by Metallica, and my stomach tightens as her phone rings.

I imagine she'll remember me—I did make quite the impression after all, and I assume she'll be receptive to a meeting up—maybe even eager. What I don't expect is for her voice to slam into my eardrum as she yells: "No, jackass, I don't want to hear the song again! Frigging call Kate if you need an audience!"

I pull the phone a little ways away from my ear. And I check the number to make sure it's the right one. It is.

Then I say, "Uh . . . hello? Is this Dee?"

There's a pause as she realizes I'm not jackass.

Then she replies, "Yes, this is Dee. Who's this?"

"Hey, it's Matthew Fisher. I work with Kate—we met at the diner this afternoon?"

Another brief pause, and then her voice lightens, "Oh yeah. Clit-boy, right?"

I chuckle deeply, not entirely sure I like that nickname, but at least I made my mark. Note to self: Use that line again.

"That's me."

"Sorry about yelling. My cousin's been up my ass all day."

My cock stirs from the ass talk, and I have to stop myself from offering to trade places with this cousin.

"What can I do for you, Matthew Fisher?"

My imagination gets crazy. And detailed. *Oh, the things she could do . . .*

For a moment I wonder if she's talking like this on purpose or if I'm just a horny mess.

I play it safe. "I was wondering if you wanted to get together sometime? For a drink?"

Let's pause right here. Because, despite my earlier complaints about the modern complexities men face when trying to hook up, I feel it's my duty to educate others, get the word out, about how to decode guy-speak. Think of me as a studlier version of Edward

Snowden or Julian Assange. Maybe I should start my own website—I'd call it DickiLeaks. On second thought, that's a shitty name. Sounds like an STD symptom.

Remember the mental game of "fuck, kill, marry" I mentioned earlier? If a man asks you to get a drink or hang out, you are squarely in the "fuck" category. Nope, don't argue—it's true. If a guy asks you for a date or dinner, maybe even a movie, you're probably in the "fuck" category, but you have potential for upward mobility.

You don't have to base your response to a dude's proposition on this information; I just thought you'd want to know.

Now, back to the phone conversation.

I can hear a smile in her voice as she accepts my invite. "I'm always up for a drink."

Up. More sexual innuendo. Definitely not my imagination. I am so getting laid.

"Cool. You free on Friday?"

Silence meets my ears for a beat, until she suggests, "How about tonight?"

Wow. Guess Delores Warren missed the chapter requiring two days' advance notice for all screwing offers.

Lucky me.

And then she elaborates. "I mean, there could be a blackout, a water shortage, aliens could finally decide to invade and enslave the entire human race . . ."

There's one I haven't heard before.

"Then we'd be shit out of luck. Why wait for Friday?"

I like the way this girl thinks. As the saying goes, "Don't put off till tomorrow anyone you could be doing today." Or . . . close enough.

"Tonight works for me," I readily agree. "What time?"

Some girls take forever and a day to get ready. It's fucking annoying. Going to the gym or the beach? Shouldn't require prep time, ladies.

"How about an hour?"

Two points for Dee—great tits *and* low maintenance. I think I'm in love.

"Sounds good." I tell her. "What's your address? I'll swing by and pick you up."

My building has private parking for tenants. Lots of New Yorkers spend thousands of dollars a month for parking spaces—only to not drive their cars because of city traffic. Auto congestion doesn't bug me; I always leave myself extra time. Like I said before—time management is key.

And another thing: I don't have a car. I drive a custom-built Ducati Monster 1100 S. I'm not looking to put on a cut and join an outlaw MC or anything, but riding is another hobby of mine. Few things in life feel as great as cruising down an open highway on a blue-skied, crisp fall day when the leaves are just starting to change. It's as close to flying as a human being can get.

I take the bike out at every available opportunity. Sometimes a girl will bitch about being cold or messing up her hair—but when all is said and done: Chicks dig motorcycles.

Delores responds, "Um . . . how about I just meet you?"

This is a smart move for a single woman. Just like you wouldn't give out your social security number online, you don't give out your address to some guy you barely know. The world is a fucked-up place, and women especially need to do everything they can to make sure the fucked up doesn't find its way to their front door.

But, unfortunately, it also means the hog is staying home tonight. I'm a little sad about that.

"Meeting up sounds good."

Before I can suggest a place, Dee takes charge. "You know Stitch's, on West 37th?"

I do know it. It's low-key with good drinks, live music, and a comfortable lounge. Because it's a Wednesday night, it won't be packed, but no bar in New York is ever empty.

"Yeah, I'm familiar with it."

"Great. I'll see you in an hour or so."

"Awesome."

After we hang up, I don't get dressed right away. I'm not picky about my clothes, like some young semi-asexual professionals, but I'm not a slob, either. I can be ready to walk out the door in seven minutes flat. So I grab the folder from my briefcase and use the extra time to finish the work reading I planned to do before bed. Because it looks like I won't be hitting the sheets any time soon—and when I do, I'm definitely not going to be alone.

I get to Stitch's early. I drink a beer at the bar, then step outside for a cigarette. Yes—I'm a smoker. Break out the hammer and nails and commence with the crucifixion.

I'm aware it's unhealthy. I don't need to see the internal organs of deceased cancer patients on those creepy-ass commercials to understand it's a bad habit—*thank you, Mayor Bloomberg*. Making me go outside doesn't stop me from lighting up—it just pisses me off. It's an inconvenience, not a deterrent.

But I'm considerate about it. I don't toss my buds on the street, I don't blow smoke in the faces of the elderly or children. Alexandra would literally slit my throat if I ever lit up anywhere near Mackenzie. Literally.

I do plan on quitting . . . eventually.

But for now, the long-term damage I might be doing to my lungs falls second to the fact that I like to smoke. It feels good. It's really just that simple. And you can keep your bar pretzels to yourself, because nothing goes better with a cold beer than a cigarette. It's as good as a mom's old-fashioned PB&J.

I snuff out my cigarette on the wall of the building and throw it into the trash can on the street. Then I pop an Altoids in my mouth. Because—like I said—I'm considerate. I don't know if Dee is a fellow smoker or not, but nobody wants to slide their tongue into another person's mouth and taste ashtray. And getting Dee's tongue in my mouth . . . among other places . . . is definitely on the schedule for tonight's festivities.

I head back in the bar and order a second beer. I take a swig and notice the front door opening. I watch as she walks in.

Did I think Delores was a hottie when I met her this afternoon? I need to get my vision checked. Because she's so much more.

Her blond hair is down, curled under at the ends, pulled back from her face with a thick black hair band. A black, tuxedo-like jacket covers her torso, with a low-cut white tube top underneath. Short, white shorts barely peek out from the bottom of the jacket, revealing long, creamy, toned legs. She finishes the look with white sky-high heels. Red lipstick accentuates her mouth.

She's gorgeous—shockingly stunning. She could easily be in a Calvin Klein campaign. Her business card isn't Charlie's Golden Ticket—it's the lottery kind—and I just hit the jackpot.

She scans the room and spots me from the doorway. I wave, coolly. She smiles back, revealing straight, shiny teeth.

"Hi," she says as she approaches.

"Hello—that jacket looks great on you." You can't go wrong by starting off with a compliment. Girls love them.

Her smile turns into a smirk as she teases, "Let me guess—'But I'd look better out of it'?"

I chuckle. "I wasn't going to say that. I would never give a line that cheesy." Then I shrug. "I was going to say, 'It'd look even better on my bedroom floor.'"

A rich, deep laugh escapes her throat. "Yeah—cause there's nothing cheesy about that."

I pull out a bar stool and she sits.

"What's your poison?" I ask.

Without a pause she answers, "Martini."

"Dirty?"

"I like my martinis just like my sex." She winks flirtatiously. "Dirty is always better."

Yes—I'm definitely in love.

The bartender comes to us, but before I can order for her, Dee starts giving specific instructions on how she wants her drink made.

"Two ounces of gin, heavy on the vermouth, just a dash of olive juice . . ."

The smooth-faced, plaid-shirted bartender, who barely looks twenty-one, seems lost. Dee notices and stands up. "You know, I'll just demonstrate—it'll be easier." She turns, hops backwards onto the bar, and swings her legs over the top—while I discreetly try to get a peek up her shorts. If she's wearing underwear, it's gotta be a thong.

My cock processes this information by straining against my jeans, hoping for a peek of his own.

Dee stands up on the business side of the bar and quickly mixes her drink, explaining every move to the unperturbed bartender. She tosses an olive into the air and catches it expertly with her mouth, before sinking the two-olived toothpick into the clear-liquid-filled glass.

She places it on the bar and motions to it with an open palm. "And there you have it—the perfect Dirty Martini."

I've always believed you can tell a lot about a person by what they drink. Beer is laid back, easy-going, or cheap, depending on the brand. Wine coolers tend to be immature or nostalgic. Cristal and Dom Pérignon imbibers are flashy and try too hard to impress—there are many champagnes that are just as expensive and exquisite, but lesser known.

What does Dee's choice of beverage tell me about her? She's complicated, with very specific, but refined, tastes. And she's out-spoken, bold without being bitchy. The kind of girl who can send back her steak to the kitchen if it's cooked wrong, in a way that doesn't make the waiter want to spit in her food.

The bartender raises his brows and gives me a friendly look. "You got a live one here, buddy."

Dee swings back over the bar as I say, "So it seems."

Once Delores is seated back on the stool, I comment, "That was impressive. So, I guess you're big on the micromanaging, huh?"

She sips her drink. "I bartended through college—it made me very particular about my poison."

I take a drag off my beer and move into the small talk portion of the evening. "Kate tells me you're a chemist. What's that like?"

She nods. "It's like playing with a chemistry set every day and getting paid to do it. I enjoy analyzing things—breaking them down to their smallest components—then fucking with them a little. Seeing what other substances they play nice with . . . or don't. The *don't* part can get pretty exciting. Sort of makes me feel like I'm on a bomb squad."

She stirs her olives in the glass. "And you're a banker?"

I nod. "More or less."

"That sounds very unexciting."

My head tilts left to right as I consider her comment. "Depends on your outlook. Some deals are a high-stakes gamble. Making money is never boring."

Dee turns in her chair, facing me.

Body language is important. Typically, a person's movements are subconscious, but understanding the feelings behind them can either guide you to the Promised Land or get your ass locked outside heaven's door. If a girl folds her arms or leans back, that generally means you're coming on too strong or she's just not interested in what you're selling. Eye contact, open arms, full frontal attention are all sure signs she's feeling you—and is hungry for more.

Her eyes quickly trail my body, head to toe. "You don't look like a banker."

I grin. "What does a banker look like?"

She scans the other patrons at the bar and in the lounge. Her gaze settles on a middle-aged, balding dude in a cheap suit, hunkered down over a double scotch, whose expression implies he's lost his life savings in a stock market crash.

Dee points at him with her crimson-nail-painted pinkie finger. "Him."

"He looks like a mortician. Or a pedophile."

She giggles and downs the rest of her martini.

Leaning close to her, I ask, "If not a banker, what do I look like?"

She smiles slowly and scrapes the olives off the toothpick with her teeth.

"You look like a Chippendales dancer."

Fabulous answer. I don't really need to explain to you why, do I?

In a low, seductive voice I say, "I do have some great moves. If banking doesn't work out, Chippendales is Plan B."

I motion to the bartender for another round. Delores watches him work closely, and he must not screw it up too badly, because she smiles when he places the drink before her.

Then, she says to me, "So . . . your buddy Drew—he's been giving my girl a hard time. Not a smart thing to do."

"Drew has a weird relationship with competition. He thrives on it, but it also pisses him off. Kate hasn't exactly been taking it easy on him, either. She brings her A-game to the office—I think she can hold her own."

"Well, you feel free to let him know he should watch his step. I'm very protective of Katie—we Ohioans stick together."

"But you're in New York now. We're 'Every Man for His-Fuck-ing-Self.' It's the second state motto—right after 'The City That Never Sleeps.'"

Her eyes shine as she laughs. And I think the first drink might be hitting her hard.

"You're cute," she tells me.

My head leans back in exasperation. "Great. *Cute.* The adjective every man wants to hear."

She laughs again, and I'm struck by how much I'm enjoying myself. Dee Warren is a cool girl—unreserved, quick-witted, funny. Even if I don't end up nailing her, the night won't be a total loss.

That's not to say I'm not dying to get her out of here and see what's—or, preferably, what's not—under those tiny shorts. But, it'd be like rich icing on an already fuck-awesome cake.

I veer back toward small talk. "You're from Ohio?"

She tastes her drink and nods. "Yes, the original Podunk, USA."

"Mmm, no love for the hometown?"

"No, Greenville was a great town to grow up in, but it's sort of like the Hotel California. People check in, but they almost never leave. If all you want out of life is to get married and have babies, it's the place to be. But . . . that wasn't what I was looking for."

"What *are* you looking for, Dee?"

She thinks for a moment before she answers. "I want . . . life. Newness. Discovery. Change. It's why I like the city so much. It's alive—never stagnant. You can walk down a block and go down that same block a week later and it'll be totally different. New people, new sights and smells—the smells aren't always good, but that's a small price to pay."

I chuckle.

Then she goes on. "My mom used to say I reminded her of a dog on a leash that never learned how to heel. Always pulling on the chain, raring to go. There's a country song with lyrics I like: 'I don't want easy, I want crazy.'" She shrugs, a little shyly. "That's me."

Everything she said—they're my favorite parts about the city I grew up in too. Life is too damn short to stay safe, to stay the same.

My cell phone buzzes, but I ignore it. Checking your phone in the middle of a conversation, even if it's with a one-nighter, is just rude. Low class.

Dee asks me what my Zodiac sign is, but I make her tell me hers first. Some people are really into signs—I've been ditched on more than one occasion by a horrified Leo or Aquarius when they found out I'm a Capricorn. Since then, I'm not above fudging my birth date if needed.

In this case, I didn't have to. Dee's a Scorpio, which is supposed to be super hot with Capricorns in the sack. Personally, I think the whole thing is a crock of shit. But, if you want to play, you've got to know the rules of the game. Including potential fouls.

Dee nurses her second drink as the conversation turns toward family and friends. Without getting too deep, she tells me about Billy, her more-like-a-brother cousin, and her single mother who raised them both. She touches on her life-long friendship with Kate Brooks and a few surprising wild-child incidents during their teen years that are just too embarrassing not to mention to Kate at the office tomorrow.

I fill her in on Drew and Steven and Alexandra and how growing up with them saved me from ever feeling like an only child. I tell her about the coolest four-year-old I know, Mackenzie, and that I would hang with that kid every day of the week if I could.

By the time I finish my fourth beer, two and a half hours have flown by. When Dee hits the bathroom, I whip out my phone.

I have six texts. They're all from Steven.

Shit. *Call of Duty.* I forgot.

They vary in their degrees of panic. Wanna see?

Dude ur late—starting without you
**

Come on, man, I'm in the shit and outnumbered. Where the hell r u?
**

Where's the goddamn aerial support? My men are dying out there!
**

Not going out like this—taking as many of them with me as I can. Ahhhhhhhh!
**

Thanks a lot, dumbass. I'm dead. If you make a move on my widow I'll haunt you.

And finally, the last one just says:

Fucker.

I laugh out loud and send him an apologetic text, telling him something suddenly came up. Steven's great at reading between the lines:

> You mean your dick suddenly came up. What happened to bros before hoes? You owe me. I expect payment in the form of babysitting hours so I can take my wife out . . . or stay in. ;)

Personally, I think he spends too much time with his wife as it is—as demonstrated by the winky face in his text.

Dee comes back from the bathroom and stands close to my chair. "You want to get out of here?"

Yes, please.

With a devastating grin, I answer, "Absolutely. You want to go to my place? I'd love to show you the view."

She glances at my crotch. "What view would that be?"

"The kind you'll never want to stop looking at, baby."

She chuckles. "I was thinking more along the lines of dancing?"

"Then we're thinking alike. Horizontal is my favorite dance."

She runs her hand up the sleeve of my black button-down shirt. "The vertical kind is a nice prelude—gets me in the mood. There's a club around the corner from my apartment. Their Wednesday night DJ is the shit. You want to come with me, Clit-boy?"

I put my hand over hers and rub my thumb slowly against it. "I don't think I like that nickname."

She shrugs unapologetically. "Too bad. You never get a second chance to make a first impression. You're Clit-boy until you give me a reason to think of you as something else."

I lean in closer. Goosebumps rise on the flesh of her chest as my breath tickles her ear. "By the end of this night, I'll have you calling me 'God.' "

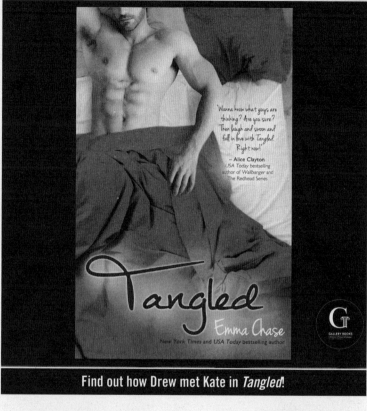